Cold Blooded Vixen:

Part One

Déjá Monét

Cold Blooded Vixen: Part One

This novel is a work of fiction. Any references to real people, events, establishments, or locales are intended only to give the fiction a sense of reality and authenticity. Other names, characters, and incidents occurring in the work are either the product of the author's imagination or are used fictitiously, as those fictionalized events and incidents that involve real persons. Any character that happens to share the name of a person who is an acquaintance of the author, past or present, is purely coincidental and is in no way intended to be an actual account involving that person.

ISBN- 13: 978-0615978482
ISBN- 10: 0615978487

Printed in the United States of America

Editor: Jamie Pender

Cover Design: Brittani Williams

www.tspubcreative.com

Photographer: Chance Green

Cover Model: Laila Zoé

Prologue

As Raquel laid back on the plush king sized bed of the Atlantis Royal Towers hotel in Paradise Island, all she could do was look up at the mirrored ceiling and ask herself how she got here. After all, this was exactly where she was supposed to be at this exact time and this exact moment, but the events that took place before her arrival did not go as planned. She went from a big time model to a murderer in just a matter of minutes.

People always say it's funny how things work themselves out and Raquel was always one to find the light at the end of the tunnel, but this time was different. This tunnel was dark and dim and she wasn't so sure if she could find her way out of this one. Raquel had to pull herself together and act as if nothing happened but how? She had to figure out something and fast!

Raquel knew by the time she arrived in the Bahamas, there were already questions being asked back home. What she didn't know was if the questions being asked were about her. She needed to make a phone call but she wasn't sure who she could trust.

With so many thoughts running through Raquel's mind, she became confused, nervous, scared, and infuriated all at the same time. All she could do was pick up the closest thing to her, which happened to be the remote and threw it against the wall. She had no idea of what to do.

"Fuck, man! I have to get my shit together! My mind is all fucked up and I'm going half crazy!" Raquel spoke out loud to herself. It was something she often did when no one else was around to talk to. "Guess I'll roll me a blunt so I can clear all these thoughts, then I can figure out to do. I shouldn't have to figure this shit out on my own but fuck it."

Raquel hopped off the bed standing only five feet three inches, naked as the day she was born. She had beautiful, caramel skin that glowed like the sunset. Even though she was small and petite, she had sexy curves that made her look like a goddess. To go along with the hazel eyes that were passed down to her from generations back, Raquel also had a head full of luscious, curly hair that she usually wore in a high bun.

Looking at her one would never question why or how she became a model—it was obvious. A killer on the other hand... No one, not even Raquel could've predicted that. But as we all know, life can take some crazy turns and you either sink or swim.

Raquel walked over to the dresser and retrieved the cigar box out of the top drawer a small trash can. With her hands full, she retreated back to the comfy bed and rolled a perfectly pearled blunt.

Smiling to herself, Raquel went into the bathroom to place on her robe. All she wanted to do at this moment was relax and feel the Island breeze and admire the palm trees and crystal clear water. She walked outside of her luxury suite and onto her private, secluded balcony.

Even though Raquel was a professional model now and she had an image to maintain, at the end of the day she was still Raquel from the Westside of Baltimore. She wasn't going to change, regardless of how much money she made. Growing up, Raquel didn't get into much trouble but she was always a pothead. She was starting to realize her love for the drug was actually a big part of how her switch from model to murderer happened so fast.

As Raquel sat down and took the first pull of her blunt, she started to think back to the beginning.

<u>Chapter 1</u>

Raquel was a young girl when she first showed an interest in modeling. Since the day she recognized the little girl in the mirror looking back at her was her own reflection, she never stopped smiling and posing. Even before she could walk, Raquel would sit in front of the mirror and make all types of faces. Her mom Brenda always thought she was just a silly baby who loved the mirror, but as Raquel got a little older, Brenda realized her daughter was a natural.

Raquel had some small successes as a child, once being featured in a kids clothing ad and a food commercial, but being from a low income family living in the Westside of Baltimore, she knew there were not many, if any opportunities to make it BIG.

She always dreamt of living and working as a well-known model in Paris, London, LA, or even New York City. Raquel always felt in her heart that she was destined for greatness. But as she looked out her bedroom window, all she could see was row homes that looked similar to the one she lived in, along with the madness which was everyday life in the city of Baltimore.

From her window she could see everything—from junkies outside shooting dope and begging for change to girls her age walking up and down the street, chasing after some teenage boy with their baby attached to their hip. Raquel always wanted something better for herself and she vowed that she would have it. And in a few years, she would get her wish.

FIVE YEARS LATER:

"Hello, everyone! I want to thank you all for coming out to celebrate with me. It really makes me happy to see so many people love me and care about my birthday, as well as my career. So let's all eat, drink, dance, and turn up in this bitch!" Raquel blurted out over the microphone as she downed a shot of Patron. It was her twenty-first birthday celebration and she was doing it big.

"You are such a hood rat, Raquel." Brenda chuckled. "Get off the stage before you hurt yourself."

Usually Raquel would have read her mother right on the spot but she was not going to let Brenda ruin her night. Not only was it Raquel's birthday but it was also her big release party. She was featured on the cover of one of the hottest magazines and her career was sure to take off once it hit shelves everywhere.

Raquel rented out one of the hottest clubs in the city. Everyone from neighborhood friends to big time business executives were in attendance.

"Hood rat?" Raquel questioned. "Girl, bye! Just because I made a few dollars don't mean I'mma change. Raquel will always be loud mouth Raquel. Ain't no press in here, these my people's! Oh but I forgot you live in bougie-ville." She added sarcastically. "Have a nice night, mom." Raquel rolled her eyes and walked off.

Brenda and Raquel never had a normal, loving mother-daughter relationship. Instead, Raquel felt as if her mother used her. Brenda always wanted something from her. If it wasn't money, then she wanted to be put in touch with this person or that person and frankly Raquel was sick of it. It was time for her to start thinking for herself now and she could care less what her mother had to say.

Raquel walked over to her good friend Sean who also doubled as her weed man. He was the only person in the world she trusted beyond a shadow of a doubt and vice versa. She was one of the few people who knew the ins and outs of Sean's business. He had everyone on the streets thinking he was just a major player in the weed game but little did everyone know, Sean had the biggest underground heroin operation in town, literally. He built a factory underneath a decoy house he owned that also had a secret tunnel for quick escape.

Sean started hustling when he was only eleven years old. He was left to run the business at the age of fifteen when his big homie Gunna was killed. All the hustlers assumed whoever killed

Gunna took over the blocks and just kept out of sight. Only his top men had knowledge of who the new king pin was and they weren't sharing any type of information. Even as a young teenage boy, Sean knew if word got out that he was on top he would meet the same fate as his mentor. So Sean decided to play the corner boy role, yet he was in charge of every man slinging drugs on the streets.

"Hey Sean, it's about time you got here! It's 1:30 in the morning! The one night I rent out our favorite spot and everybody in here smoking weed ya ass is late! You could be in here making my birthday money!" Raquel barked.

All Sean could do is laugh. Raquel was a spitfire but he loved that about her. He had a crush on Raquel since the first day they met but he never tried anything with her. As she continued to be a regular customer of his, the two of them became good friends.

Raquel wasn't like most women. Not only was she beautiful but she was intelligent and a go getter just like he was. He never tried anything with Raquel mainly because of the nine year age difference between them. When they first met, she was only seventeen years old and Sean couldn't look past that.

"Girl, calm down. I had to take care of something. I'm here now though so chill lil' mama," Sean said smoothly.

Raquel blushed and playfully punched Sean in the chest. He always could make her smile even on her worst day. She always hoped for more between them but she figured he wasn't interested since he never made a move. Not to mention he had a bitch for a girlfriend named Keema.

Keema was always jealous and suspicious of Sean and Raquel's friendship, but Raquel could care less about her feelings.

"Anyway... Wassup? You by yourself or did you bring Keema with you?" Raquel said being smart.

Sean just laughed and shook his head. He couldn't understand what it was with women. All he wanted was for two of them to get along but he knew that was impossible.

"Now you know Keema ain't here. I see this party live though, you got everybody in here. You looking good in your all black dress too." Sean playfully pinched Raquel's cheek.

"STOP BEFORE YOU MESS UP MY MAKEUP SEAN!" Raquel yelled.

Sean laughed at how dramatic Raquel was being. He didn't see the big fuss over makeup. He thought most woman could do without it anyway. "Okay Miss Sensitive, let's go smoke."

Raquel grabbed Sean by the hand and walked over to the back of the club where she had her own special VIP section.

"Here. I got you something for you." Sean said as he handed Raquel a small gift bag as they sat.

Raquel looked inside and found a black gift box. As she opened the box Raquel was beyond surprised! Her jaw dropped and her eyes opened as wide as saucers. Inside the box was the all-white diamond incrusted Chanel watch she saw while they went mall hopping last week. They went from Towson Town Center to Columbia Mall, over to Arundel Mills and ended the day with Tysons Corner. She couldn't even remember where she saw the watch but she was glad Sean did. All she remembered was quickly glancing at it through a window of some jewelry store.

"So I guess you like it?" Sean asked.

Raquel woke up out of her daze and answered, "Of course! How did you... when did...?" She couldn't even form a complete sentence. "Aww... Thank you, Sean!" Raquel jumped up and gave Sean a hug and kiss on the cheek. He never bought her anything this expensive before but she figured because it was her twenty-first birthday, he wanted to give her something special.

They remained in the VIP section all night, only leaving a few times to mingle with the crowd. They smoked, drank, and laughed for hours until the party was over. As the club started to clear out, they both begin to gather themselves and prepare to exit the club. Sean stood up and extended his hand to help Raquel onto her feet when he heard a voice from behind him.

"Let that drunk bitch get up by herself."

It was no one other than Keema. She was the reason he was late to Raquel's party in the first place. Keema did not want her man out celebrating with the woman she thought was interested in him while she sat at home alone.

"What you say?" Raquel questioned as she stood up from her seat, removing her leopard print YSL heels. Although Raquel was drunk she was always ready for a good fight. She loved to use her boxing skills on people who tested her.

"I said let that…" Keema started.

And before she could finish her sentence, Raquel charged over to Keema and hit her with a right hook, knocking her instantly to the floor. Jumping on top of her, Raquel continued to punch Keema in the face alternating between fists.

"Ay, ay!" Sean yelled as he rushed over to the two women. He pulled tiny Raquel off of Keema's five foot seven, athletic built frame. Regardless of a person's size, Raquel wouldn't back down for anything. She did not put up with anyone disrespecting her, not even Brenda.

Raquel felt not only did Keema come to her party and disrespect her, but she was also with the man Raquel wanted so she used this opportunity to release all her pent up anger.

"YO STOP! CALM DOWN!" Sean shouted, holding Raquel in an attempt to restrain her. He then turned his attention to Keema, "And what the fuck is wrong with you coming up in here starting shit?"

"I told you I didn't want you to come here but you came anyway! I'm sick of this! I'm sick of y'all pretending like you're just friends. I saw y'all over there! Don't lie!" Keema cried hysterically.

Sean was fed up at this point. He wasn't in the mood to deal with Keema or her bullshit and he didn't like to make a scene with the line of business he was in. "Go home, yo. I'll see you in the morning. Raquel, let's go."

And just like that, Sean left Keema standing there, alone.

"My guess is you weren't expecting to get your ass whooped but from the looks of that swollen eye and busted lip you were wrong. Goodnight, you dumb ass bitch." Raquel spewed as she walked past Keema and out the door with Sean.

As soon as they were outside the club and out of Keema's sight, Raquel snatched away from Sean and started to walk off.

"Raquel! Aye yo Raquel wait up!" Sean yelled running behind her.

Ignoring him, she walked faster. She was tired of the drama between Sean and Keema. Since their shenanigans ruined her night, she didn't want to talk to him either. *This is some bullshit,* she thought.

Raquel sighed in annoyance as she heard her cell phone going off. She rolled her eyes seeing her mother's name on the caller ID. "I'll call you back!" she said curtly, disconnecting the line before anything else could be said. She was in no mood to explain what had just taken place, especially not to Brenda.

"Yo, what's wrong?" Sean started, quickly catching up to Raquel despite her best efforts to ditch him. "Why you mad at me? I didn't know she was coming." He knew it was a weak explanation but he hated when Raquel was mad at him.

Raquel suddenly whirled around to face him. "You should have more control over that bitch. Why would you tell her where you was going in the first place?" She held a hand up as he started to speak, effectively cutting him off. "You know what? Just leave me the fuck alone. I have a busy day tomorrow!" She wasn't interested in anything Sean had to say. She was done for the night.

"Well, at least let me drive you home." Sean suggested, refusing to give up so easily. "I'm sorry, Ra. What you want me to do?" Sean asked looking Raquel dead in her eyes.

Without thinking, in a drunken high rage, Raquel blurted out, "I want you to leave that ratchet ass hoe alone and be with me!" As soon as the words left Raquel's mouth she instantly regretted them.

Oh shit! I didn't mean to say that out loud. Damn you, Patron! Raquel thought to herself. Embarrassed by her outburst, she attempted to turn around and walk away but before she could, Sean quickly grabbed her arm, pulled her in close and kissed her passionately.

Raquel instantly felt so safe and secure with his strong arms wrapped tightly around her. She never thought this day would happen and now that it was, she wasn't sure how she felt about it.

"So you gonna let me take you home, Ra?" Sean asked again as he broke their kiss.

Raquel didn't know what to do. She just quietly shook her head 'yes' and handed Sean her keys.

***

The twenty five minute ride from downtown to Raquel's home in Owings Mills was completely silent. There was not a bit of conversation, just 92Q playing slow jams on the radio. Raquel just sat back in the passenger seat of her car and enjoyed the crisp night air through the slightly cracked window as she replayed the events of tonight in her head.

When they finally arrived, Sean pulled up the driveway and parked in the garage. They both got out and entered Raquel's house through the garage door entrance that led into the kitchen. Raquel went upstairs to shower while Sean went into the kitchen grabbed a Corona out of the refrigerator. He then walked over to the living room and plopped down on Raquel's sofa and turned on her seventy inch television to catch up on the news.

Sean drank his beer as he began to roll a blunt. He knew once Raquel was out of the shower that would be the first thing she wanted.

Meanwhile, Raquel was upstairs fresh out the shower with nothing on but her silk black robe. She was sitting on the edge of the bed still trying to wrap her head around the events that took place. She wanted to call her best friend Keisha and vent but she was away on her honeymoon with her new husband Dre. Raquel didn't know much about Dre since Keisha kept him away from everyone, which she never understood why. He was cool from what she could see, and he even sold her weed a few times.

For most of their lives Raquel and Keisha lived only a few doors down from each other, but since Keisha's mom was a dope fiend she spent most of her time at Raquel's house. They became close like sisters. Keisha was always the first person Raquel would run to when she needed to talk and now that she was unavailable, Raquel didn't know what to do.

"I can't believe the nerve of that bitch Keema. Then you had the nerve to tell this man you want him?! What were you thinking Raquel?!" she spoke out loud to herself.

She had no idea what Sean was downstairs thinking. *Did he kiss me because we were fucked up? Or does he actually like me? What about Keema? Did he leave and go home to her?* All these different thoughts were running through Raquel's head so she figured it was time to go downstairs and face the music. She put on her brave face and headed for the stairs.

As Raquel approached the top of the steps, she heard the television which led her to believe Sean was still there. Sean came and went as he pleased and whenever he left her home he always made sure to turn everything off.

When she continued down the stairs, she saw Sean sitting there on her couch with the remote in his hand flipping through channels. He looked damn good sitting there with the light of the television reflecting off his skin. Sean stood about six feet tall. He had a smooth, milk chocolate complexion with the prettiest brown eyes that shined like marbles. He had deep waves in his hair, he always kept a fresh shape up and His full, long beard was always neatly trimmed.

Sean didn't work out a lot but he had a natural muscular build. His smile could melt the panties off most women, including Raquel but she would never let him know it. She didn't throw herself at men or act promiscuous. She always thought those things would one day attract Sean to her and now it seemed as if it was finally happening.

Raquel walked into the living room and sat on the loveseat across from Sean.

"Damn. It's like that? You can't sit next to me now? I got something for you." Sean picked up the blunt he'd rolled and waved it in the air teasing her.

Raquel chuckled at how well he knew her. Taking a seat next to him, she snatched the blunt from his hand, and lit it taking a long drag.

Sean grabbed Raquel's feet and began to massage them one by one. This took Raquel by surprise. They never had this type of intimate contact with each other before. Neither one of them said a word... they just looked into each other's eyes while Sean continued the massage.

After a few minutes, Raquel started to feel uncomfortable. Not because Sean was massaging her feet, but because she wanted him in a totally different way than before. A slight tingle down Raquel's spine shocked her back into reality. She quickly pulled her feet out of Sean's hands and passed him the blunt.

"What's wrong Ra? You don't like my foot massage?" Sean asked playfully as he inhaled the smoke.

"This is weird." Raquel admitted. She kept her head down, avoiding making any eye contact with him. "I don't see how you over there acting like tonight wasn't a huge disaster."

"Raquel, I've been attracted to you since the first day I saw you," he started, "I never made a move because you were young. Then by the time you were old enough, we were already cool and I didn't wanna fuck that up."

Sean was tired of hiding his feelings for Raquel. She was a grown woman now and since she showed some type of interest in him, he decided to be upfront. He put the blunt in the ashtray and kneeled down in front of Raquel and lifted her chin so they were eye to eye.

"Now did you mean what you said tonight? Do you want to be with me, Raquel?" Sean questioned with all sincerity.

Raquel could not believe what she just heard. Did the man she'd wanted all of these years finally ask her to be with him? Was it a rhetorical question?

The whole night was going great until Keema showed up and now everything was moving so fast and Raquel couldn't process it quickly enough.

"I don't know, Sean, this is crazy," Raquel answered as she lowered her head again. She was confused and didn't know if she meant it or not.

"Well maybe this will help you make up your mind." Sean untied Raquel's robe, gently pushing her back on the couch and picking up both of her legs. He slightly pulled her off the couch until he was looking directly at her sweet spot as her full round ass hung partially off the couch.

Raquel's adrenaline began to rush and her sweet spot instantly became wet and sticky as she was turned on. Sean opened her legs and went in tongue first starting with just the clitoris. He worked his tongue so fast and precise that Raquel immediately screamed out with pleasure.

"Oh shit, Sean, what are you doing?" Raquel moaned.

Sean didn't stop to answer her, he just simply began to lick and suck every single inch of her pussy leaving no spot untouched, loving every bit of it. Raquel had the prettiest pussy he had ever seen. She kept it completely bald and it smelled like rose infused water. It was so wet and Raquel matched his movements by grinding her pussy right into his mouth with every motion.

Just when Raquel thought it couldn't get any better, Sean took his fingers, opened up her sweet spot, and slid his long wet tongue in and out, working it as if it could penetrate her. Within seconds Raquel released her sweet juices all over Sean's face along with loud screams of passion.

Raquel didn't just cum, her juices flowed like a river and Sean enjoyed every drop as if he were drinking water from a fountain. She tasted so sweet and he loved all the noises and faces she made. This was a day Sean had been waiting on for years.

While Raquel laid on the couch trying to catch her breath, Sean walked over to the refrigerator to grab another beer. He rejoined Raquel on the couch and asked, "So did that help you at all?"

Raquel was still at a loss for words, Sean had her hypnotized. All she could do was jump onto his lap and kiss him like he was going off to war. She could taste her sweet juices on his lips and tongue and that turned her on even more.

"To be honest Sean, I always wanted to be with you but I never thought you were interested. Then there's Keema, what about her?" Raquel inquired.

Sean didn't respond right away. It wasn't something he'd actually thought about. He did want to be with Raquel but he was currently in a relationship and living with Keema.

Damn, Raquel thought, noticing Sean's hesitation to answer the question at hand. She got up and began to walk away.

"Wait Ra!" Sean pleaded with a sense of urgency. "Just answer my question and then we can figure out the rest. Do you want to be with me?"

"Yes." she simply answered. No sooner than the words escaped her lips, Sean scooped her off her feet and carried her into the bedroom where the two spent the rest of the night sleeping peacefully cuddled in each other's arms.

Chapter 2

The next morning Sean woke up at 8:26 am to find Raquel still sleeping. He couldn't help but to lay there and admire her beauty. To him, she was perfect. He softly ran his finger down the bridge of her nose, stopping at her chin.

Raquel smiled, feeling his gentle touch and opened her eyes.

"Good morning beautiful." Sean said.

Raquel greeted him with a good morning kiss and this time she took complete control. She rolled Sean onto his back and climbed on top of him, kissing him while stroking his dick with one hand. Raquel's sweet spot started to become wet as she felt his thick long dick grow bigger and bigger in her hand.

When Sean was completely hard, Raquel wasted no time straddling him, sliding his thick long shaft in between her tight wet walls. As she slid further down his manhood they both let out moans of pleasure. She began to ride him slowly as Sean grinded his hips underneath her. Raquel moved up and down while rolling her hips in small circular motions. Sean began to get so into it that he grabbed Raquel by the hips and began to thrust rapidly in and out of her while she continued to ride him. He then flipped Raquel onto her side, lifted her leg in the air and fucked her as hard as he could.

"Damn Sean, this feels so good! Ohh ohh ohhhh!!!" Raquel cried out.

"You feel so good Ra, I want you to be mine forever." Sean said softly as he slowed his rhythm and began to do long slow strokes.

"Mmmm!!! Yes I'll be yours Sean. Yes!" Raquel spoke between moans.

Without warning Sean flipped Raquel over on all four and began to hit it doggie style. He watched his thick, black, ten and a half inch dick slide in and out of her tight pussy which almost made him climax before he was ready. Feeling the end of their passionate fuck session nearing, Sean started to pump faster and harder as he held onto Raquel's shoulders.

"Oh, baby, yes, right there! Yeah Sean, fuck me harder, I'm about to cum!" Raquel shouted.

Right before the hot sticky semen left the tip of his dick, Sean pulled out and released himself on the sheets. They both collapsed on the bed and Sean cuddled up behind her holding her close.

After a few moments of pure bliss, Raquel turned to face Sean and asked him, "What are we doing Sean?" They had now taken things to a whole new level and she wanted them to be on the same page.

Sean looked at Raquel and playfully said, "You seem like you had a pretty good idea of what you were doing. Do you really need an answer?" He asked as he smacked Raquel on the ass but by the look on her face, he knew she was in no joking mood. He realized she was serious and he wanted to put her mind at ease.

"Look, you said you mine, right? I'mma handle Keema. You don't have nothing to worry about baby. It's about us now. I love you Raquel."

Raquel tongued Sean down, happy that they were finally going to give their love a chance.

After taking Sean to pick up his car, Raquel returned home, changed the sheets on the bed and hopped in the shower. The hot steamy water felt like heaven on her sore aching body. After a night of fighting and wild morning sex, the hot shower was exactly what she needed.

Raquel washed her naked body and shampooed her hair before stepping out the shower. She dried her wet, curly hair with a towel and quickly placed it up in a high bun and left it to dry. She rubbed some lotion onto her silky smooth skin and put on a black lace bra and panty set. Raquel was happy to know she would see her best friend Keisha today. She still had about an hour to waste before Keisha's plane landed at noon so she sat on her bed and rolled a nice blunt to start her day off.

When she finished, Raquel went over to her closet and began to pack for the busy few days ahead of her. The release party was over and done with so now it was time to get back to work. Tomorrow was the day she would begin on her journey to stardom. She had two meetings along with a photo shoot in hot, sunny Los Angeles and she couldn't wait.

After about thirty minutes of picking clothes, shoes, makeup, jewelry, purses, toiletries, and anything else she could think of, Raquel was tired and decided she was done. She hated packing because she never knew what to bring. She thought if she didn't bring it she might need it so she *always* over packed.

Oh well. Raquel threw on a pair of jeans, t-shirt, and slipped her pretty size seven feet into her favorite Chanel wedges. *Can't forget this,* she thought as her eyes settled on the Chanel watch her man had given her. She actually giggled at the thought of referring to Sean as her "man". It was still all very new and unreal to her. Not to mention, Sean still had a woman at home.

Fuck her, Raquel smiled. She had already decided not to let that bother her. It wasn't like Keema was any real competition anyway. Raquel has never been a hater so she could admit that

Keema was very attractive. She had pecan brown skin, a coke bottle figure, and shoulder length hair that was cut into a bob with a Chinese bang. It matched perfectly with her squinted brown eyes, but even with all that she was still no Raquel. Keema was a true hood rat who hooked her claws into Sean with her sex appeal, not her intellect and for that reason alone Raquel felt secure.

All dressed and ready to go, Raquel grabbed her things and headed for the garage. She took her keys off the key rack and got into her all black 2014 Cadillac Escalade. It was her newest toy and her new favorite vehicle to drive. She still loved her old car, a 2009 BMW 750 Li, but she'd always had a thing for trucks. She loved riding around in big boy shit.

The reaction she got when she pulled up, music blasting with every single window tinted out was *priceless*. People couldn't believe a petite woman like her was whipping a car so big. It made her feel like the boss she was.

Raquel reached into her glove compartment and hit a small button that opened a secret compartment. She pulled out a lighter and some smoke deodorizing spray to mask the smell, and headed for the airport. As Tupac blared through her speakers, all Raquel could think about was Sean. The words of the song currently playing reminded her of last night.

"I'd rather be ya N-I-G-G-A, so we can get drunk and smoke weed all day. It don't matter if you lonely baby, you need a thug in your life, cause busters ain't loving you right."

That's exactly how the night got started. Just me and my homeboy chilling as usual and now look at us, Raquel thought to herself with a laugh.

By the time Raquel finished daydreaming, she was on I-95 approaching the BWI Airport. Keisha said she would call after they got their luggage so Raquel drove in circles around the airport to avoid being harassed by security.

Just as she was about to make her third round, her phone rang and it was Keisha.

"Hey bitch, where y'all at?!" Raquel asked excited.

"We standing right out front... soon as you pull up." Keisha informed.

"Alright." In no time Raquel looped back around to the entrance. She couldn't park and jump out of her truck fast enough. She missed having her smoking partner and confidant around. There was so much to fill Keisha in on.

"Hey Ra Ra!" Keisha yelled out as she saw her BFF run towards her. They embraced each other like they were separated for years.

"Wassup baby girl. How you doing?" Dre asked Raquel with a stupid expression on his face.

"I'm good." She replied as she walked back towards the truck with her best friend. As Dre put the bags in the back, Raquel couldn't hold it in any longer. "Bitch, I got some shit to tell you and it can't wait!" she said in whisper so Dre couldn't hear.

"Well let's go to Mo's and rap then." Keisha suggested.

Mo's was their go to spot when they just wanted to chill and unwind.

"Hell yea, bitch. I definitely need a drink so I guess Mo's it is!" Raquel replied excited.

After dropping Dre off at the house he and Keisha shared in The Village, the two women continued down Edmondson Ave and headed downtown to Mo's. On the way there, Keisha filled Raquel in on her honeymoon in Jamaica. From the way she described the beautiful crystal clear water, palm trees, and exquisite cuisine, it sounded like a wonderful place to spend time with the person you loved.

Raquel started to think of Sean and if they would ever get to that place in their relationship. She giggled at the idea of being Mrs. Sean Crosby.

"What's so funny whore?" Keisha questioned Raquel, knocking her from her thoughts.

"Nothing I was just thinking about something." she said quickly brushing her off.

"Mmm hmm… Well don't be mad when I'm getting my drink on not listening to your dry ass story."

"Girl please! There's nothing dry about this story. You'll be so into it you might forget the drinks are there."

Raquel could tell by the look on her friend's face that she had Keisha's full attention.

***

Sean didn't know how he was going to face Keema once he got home.

I really fucked up this time, he thought. Not only did he go to Raquel's party after Keema asked him not to, but he also left his girl standing alone in the club after she got her ass beat *and* spent the night with the person Keema hated the most.

Hearing his phone going off again, Sean decided to ignore it. He knew without checking the caller ID the person on the other line was Keema. She had been calling and texting him all night and he was sure she wasn't about to give up now.

All Sean wanted to do was enjoy the ride home in peace as he tried to figure out his next move. He was ready to leave his relationship with Keema behind. He was tired of her and the bullshit that came along with her. All she did was party and ask him for money and weed. The pussy was good but he wanted something more than that. Sean was now thirty years old and ready to settle down and he believed Raquel was the perfect woman to do that with.

As soon as Sean parked and entered the house Keema came running down the stairs.

"OH NOW YOU WANNA COME HOME?! WHERE THE FUCK YOU BEEN ALL NIGHT, NIGGA? WITH YOUR SO CALLED FRIEND YOU LEFT ME FOR AFTER I CAME DOWN THERE TO BRING YOUR ASS HOME WITH ME WHERE YOU *SHOULD HAVE* BEEN IN THE FIRST PLACE?!" Keema screamed at the top of her lungs.

Sean was in no mood for the dramatics. All he wanted to do was tell her it was over and leave. He was even going to let her keep their home in Patterson Park. As Sean continued to ignore her, he walked into the living room and was devastated by what he saw; Keema destroyed everything.

Their once all white living room now looked like the scene of a bloody massacre. Keema spray painted streaks of red all over the white carpet and the all-white furniture. She ripped up all of their pictures and trashed his DVD collection along with the speakers for the surround sound. He didn't even want to imagine what the rest of the house looked like. All he wanted to do was leave before he did something he would regret.

Going into the kitchen, he grabbed a couple of black trash bags from the pantry and headed up stairs to grab some clothes to take with him.

"Oh, so you leaving now Sean? You gonna go play house with your precious Ra?" Keema kept nagging on and on as Sean continued to throw whatever he could find into the trash bags. She was beginning to get under Sean's skin with her ranting and raving and before Sean knew it he snapped!

"Yea I'm leaving ya no good trifling ass! You can have this fucking house! I hope you die in this muthafucka, you stinking ass hoe!" Sean blurted out as the blood boiled in his veins. He had been holding in so much when it came to Keema and their relationship and he simply couldn't do it anymore.

Keema was surprised Sean went off on her like that. With all the things she did in the past not once did Sean disrespect her the way he just did, so she figured she would throw daggers right back.

"Well that's fine. I wish you two the best of luck. Tell Raquel I hope she likes playing step mommy because I'M PREGNANT, BITCH!" Keema said as she threw a shoe at Sean's head to further prove her point.

Sean stood there completely stunned. He could not believe what he just heard. It was as if time stopped for a moment. In a matter of seconds his life had completely changed. Not only was this crazy bitch pregnant with his seed but he was going to lose Raquel. There was no way she was going to accept this. Keema had just dropped the biggest bomb on him ever and Sean was devastated.

"What did you say?" Sean said looking at Keema in disbelief. He wanted to make sure he heard her correctly, even though there was no way to misinterpret her statement.

Keema stood there with her hands on her hips and repeated herself with nothing but attitude, "I said I'm PREGNANT!" She could see the shock and devastation on his face and was sure that she had won.

***

Raquel and Keisha walked into Mo's and headed straight for the bar. They took their seats and waited for the server to take their drink order.

"So how was your party, bestie? I wish I could have been there." Keisha said, knowing she missed a big event.

Now was the time to fill Keisha in on everything she missed while on her honeymoon. "Well, the party was great, everyone showed up and we had a good time. We all ate, drank, danced, smoked, you know how we do. But yo, shit got real when Keema showed up." Raquel paused and waited for her friend's reaction.

"Keema? Sean's Keema?" Keisha asked in confusion.

"Yes bitch. *That* Keema and long story short, I whooped her ass!" Raquel laughed.

"Wait, wait! Hold up a second. What the fuck happened? Short story my ass." Keisha wanted the full story, no summaries. She lived for a story with juicy details.

"She was mad because Sean came to the party and she didn't want him to… You know, blah blah… the same drama as always. But that bitch showed up and got the popping off at the mouth and I popped her ass right in it."

Keisha burst out with laughter. She knew Keema had it coming. She was surprised her best friend hadn't beat the bitch up months ago.

"That's not what I wanted to talk to you about though. It's something else." Raquel was a little nervous about telling her judgmental friend about her and Sean. Keisha always had something to say about the men she dated but Raquel had to tell someone. "Me and Sean are kinda together now." Raquel confessed.

"BITCH, YOU LYING!" Keisha shouted out. She was so loud the majority of the people in the crowded restaurant looked in their direction to see what all the commotion was. Keisha didn't care how loud she was and Raquel was accustomed to being embarrassed by her ghetto ass friend.

"Yes we finally told each other how we feel." She nodded. "And he said he would leave Keema so we could be together. He should be home telling that ratchet ass hoe now. Oh and he gave me this Chanel watch for my birthday," Raquel bragged playfully, holding out her wrist.

Keisha was in complete shock and she had good reason to be. Keema was Dre's first cousin, and according to him, Keema was pregnant with Sean's baby! Keisha was pretty sure her friend didn't know her new man was expecting a baby by his old bitch. If Raquel did, she was sure that she'd have mentioned it by now.

Keisha hadn't seen Ra happy with a man in years, so she thought it was best to keep her mouth closed until she got more information on the "baby" situation. She would make sure to ask her husband as soon as she got home.

"Damn, bitch! Are you going to say anything?" Raquel questioned her friend. She was sure Keisha would have a lot to say once she dropped the news but surprisingly she didn't say a word. Before Keisha could open her mouth to say anything the bartender came to take their order.

"Umm... we'll have two double shots of Patron and a pound of steamed shrimp please." Raquel politely requested.

After placing the order, Raquel turned back to her friend as she waited for an answer.

"You know I'm happy for you girl I'm just shocked." Keisha lied, finally finding her voice. "Did y'all fuck? Was it good?" She quickly changed the subject in an attempt to recompose herself.

Raquel knew her nosy ass friend would ask her that if nothing else. "Yes bitch and it was fucking HUGE!" she answered as they slapped high fives.

The two friends sat at the bar in Mo's drinking and eating, talking about all the trouble they got into over the years. Their good conversation and laughter was interrupted by the ringing of Keisha's cell phone. It was a text message from Dre asking when she was coming home. It was only four o'clock in the afternoon but they were newlyweds so Keisha decided to go home to her man. The ladies wrapped things up, paid the tab, and headed out the restaurant.

After dropping Keisha off, Raquel headed back home to Owings Mills. When she arrived she expected to see Sean or see that he had at least been there but there was no sign of him. Everything was just the way she left it. She reached into her purse and pulled out her cell phone and tried to call Sean but no answer.

"He'll call me back." Raquel assured herself. She then walked up the stairs, undressed, and slipped on a t-shirt that belonged to Sean. He had a lot of his stuff there. Whenever he needed to get away from Keema or the street life, he would often come to Ra's crib.

Raquel turned on the tube and began to enjoy her favorite pastime, which was smoking weed. As she sat in bed watching *Paid in Full,* her mind started to wander. It had been almost two hours since she tried to call Sean and he hadn't called or texted back which was unusual.

Maybe he's taking care of business, she thought. *He'll probably call or come by when he gets the chance. He promised me that I had nothing to worry about and I'm gonna believe him.*

Raquel went downstairs into the kitchen and made a big bowl of Froot Loops to satisfy her munchies and returned upstairs. After eating her snack Raquel sat and watched television, waiting on Sean's call until she fell asleep.

***

Sean gathered his things, jumped into his Range Rover, and drove around trying to clear his mind. He also needed to make a couple of stops and see a few people.

After handling his business, Sean made his way to The Aloft Hotel at National Harbor. He often came to this hotel when he needed to escape his life in Baltimore. Inside his room, he sat on the edge of the bed and looked down at his cell phone. He had two missed calls from his new love but he couldn't face her right now.

How the fuck am I gonna tell her this shit? He finally had the chance to be with the woman he dreamed of and now his chances were ruined. Sean was trying to come up with the right words to tell Raquel but he knew no matter what he said, it wasn't going to be easy. Even if she could look past the baby, he wasn't sure if Ra could ever accept Keema being a permanent fixture in his life. Sean figured if he could avoid Raquel for the remainder of the day that would buy him some time to straighten some things out. He knew she was going out of town on business and he would have a plan together by the time she came back to Baltimore.

Sean pulled out a bag of weed along with a Dutch and began to roll up. After he finished, he walked into the living room, opened the sliding glass door and stepped outside onto the balcony. He reached in this pocket for a lighter and sparked his perfectly rolled blunt blowing out a cloud of smoke.

Sean just wanted to relax and clear his mind of all the drama. He was away from the streets as well as Keema so he wanted to enjoy the moment. The view of the Potomac River and the warm night breeze was exactly what he needed. It was like a mini vacation for him, being a little over an hour away from home. After a good night's sleep he would think about how he would tell Raquel. He also needed to find a place to stay because the hotel thing wasn't for him and neither was living with Keema.

Sean went back into the suite, laid on the bed and began to think of how to get himself out of the mess he created. He decided to text Raquel back so she wouldn't start to worry.

Hey baby sorry I missed your calls. I'm in DC handling some business. Have a safe flight 2morrow, love u Ra

-Sean

Sean turned his phone off just in case Raquel was still awake. He didn't want to ignore another call from her, especially after he just hit her phone. He just laid in bed lost in his thoughts until he fell into a deep sleep.

***

"So you finally decided to come home, huh?" Dre asked annoyed when Keisha strolled into the house. He was sitting in the living room waiting for her return.

"I'm sorry baby. Raquel needed to vent and tell me all about her party and the drama that..."

Keisha didn't even see it coming. Quicker than lightning, Dre had gotten up and slapped her across the face. He'd hit her so hard that she spun and hit the carpeted floor.

"Get up bitch!" Dre yelled.

Truthfully, this wasn't anything out of the ordinary. Even still Keisha thought Dre had finally changed. He had been so nice, loving, and supportive after he caused her to miscarry a few months ago and now he'd flipped like a light switch.

Keisha couldn't believe this was happening again. She had doubts about getting married to Dre because of their history but she really believed he loved her and wouldn't hurt her ever again. As she tried to stand on her feet Dre kicked Keisha in her stomach sending her into complete shock. The pain was unbearable. It was like déjá vu. He kicked her in the same spot when she told him she was two months pregnant with his child. Keisha left Dre after the miscarriage but after weeks and weeks of begging along with all the wining and dining she took him back.

Everything was perfect after they got back together. Dre seemed like a different man. He cooked and cleaned for her, ran her bath water, and constantly apologized for causing her to lose their unborn child, but now she could see it was all an act. They were fresh off their honeymoon and he was turning into Mr. Hyde.

Keisha lay balled up on the floor crying out in pain. Dre walked over to Keisha, picked her up off the floor, and carried her upstairs. She was terrified. She had no idea what this man was about to do to her. He walked into the bedroom, sat Keisha on the bed and headed for the bathroom where he ran a hot bath for her. He then went back into the room where he found Keisha with a swollen check, bent over holding her stomach, tears streaming down her face.

"I'm sorry baby girl, I was just mad. I thought you might wanna spend our first night as a married couple home with me but you rather go out with shorty. You fucking her or something?"

Keisha couldn't believe her ears. Was this nigga fucking crazy?! She simply shook her head 'no', not saying a word to avoid an argument. She was in too much pain to fight verbally or otherwise.

"I wouldn't be surprised. I mean you always with that bitch. You eating her pussy?" Dre continued.

"No. It won't happen again baby, sorry." Keisha softly whispered.

"It better not. Now take off ya clothes and get in the tub!" he ordered.

Keisha slowly rose to her feet and began to undress. She removed her shoes and clothes as Dre watched, becoming erect at the sight. He grabbed the bulge in his pants and walked over to his new bride, jamming his tongue down her throat while playing with her clit.

Keisha was nowhere near turned on. After the beating Dre just put on her, she was in no mood for sex. Every kiss and touch from Dre at that moment repulsed her, but she knew if she denied him that would send him into another rage. She could taste the 1738 he had been drinking as he continued to kiss her.

Dre dropped his pants, pushed Keisha against the wall and violently jammed his dick in her. "Bitch, this is my pussy. If I find out you giving it away, I'll fucking kill you." Dre said as he fucked Keisha roughly against the wall, one hand around her neck as she silently cried. He pumped as fast and hard as he could, ensuring he got his point across. He felt so in control, Keisha was nothing but property to him. He loved her in his own way but that came second to his controlling and abusive ways.

After three long minutes of rough angry sex, Dre released his semen inside of Keisha and she was glad it was finally over. He pulled up his clothes, headed down the stairs, and left out the front door. Keisha was in disbelief. She wanted to call Raquel but she didn't want to bother her with this drama before she left for her big business trip. Plus she didn't know how to tell Raquel. She always kept the abuse to herself.

Keisha became very good at covering up bruises or going on "vacations" when she had black eyes, swollen lips or anything else she couldn't disguise. She never even told her best friend about the pregnancy or the miscarriage. Keisha went into the bathroom, stepped into the lukewarm water and started to think of how she was going to leave Dre— and for good this time. She didn't care that they were just married a few days ago; she was not going to be his punching bag anymore.

Chapter 3

The next morning Raquel was awakened at 6:30am by the sound of her alarm clock.

BEEP!! BEEP!! BEEP!! BEEP!!

Raquel hit the off button and sat up in her bed to avoid falling back asleep. Today was the day she would fly to Los Angeles and begin a new venture in her career. Even though everything was confirmed through Raquel's agent and she had her plane tickets and itinerary, it was all so surreal to her. She could not believe her dream was finally coming true.

Times like this made Raquel grateful for how Brenda treated her. The harshness and critique she received from her mother over the years always made Raquel want more for herself. She always worked hard and never gave up, even after numerous rejections. There were many times Raquel thought she would never make to this level but now that it had, she never wanted it to end.

Not too long ago Raquel was only hosting parties and had small features in slightly popular magazines. But now that she was featured on a well-known magazine cover, and was being requested to be the face of several brands. Her big break came about a year ago when she starred as the leading lady in a music video of an upcoming rap artist from Baltimore that received millions of views online.

It all happened so fast. It seemed as if she blinked and next thing she knew, Raquel was working with a legit agent. Even though she was living very comfortably, her new business ventures now put her in another tax bracket. Her agent Charles made sure Raquel was well taken care of because the more money she made, he made.

Raquel got out of bed and went into the bathroom to shower and brush her teeth. She was not a morning person and even though this was one of the most important days of her life, today was no different. As she looked at her reflection in the mirror, she was grateful for her flawless skin. Not a bit of makeup was going to touch her face until she was in LA, except her brows of course. Beating face to go sit on a plane just to have it taken off and re-done was pointless to her.

One thing she was never too tired to do was roll a nice blunt which she needed for the five and a half hour plane ride. Raquel quickly rolled up, threw on a pair of jean shorts, socks, and black combat boots, along with a tank top and hoodie. She knew once she arrived in LA the weather would be much warmer than it was in Baltimore, so she put a pair of sandals in her purse and would just remove her hoodie and wear the tank top once she arrived.

Raquel pulled her luggage out the closet and placed the bags at the top of the stairs. She went back into her room to grab the other things she needed before she drove herself to the airport.

"Keys? Check. Blunt, purse, blanket, sunglasses, headphones, phone and charger? Check!" Raquel reassured herself. "Well that's everything. Let's go." She didn't want to leave her new whip in parking garage so she threw her things in the BMW and started her normal driving routine.

Once again, Raquel enjoyed her blunt while listening to some music. Riding and smoking was one of Raquel's favorite things to do, it helped to ease her mind. Unlike most people, Raquel didn't always smoke to get high. For her it was more for relaxation and creativity.

After arriving at the airport, Raquel parked her car in the garage and put out the blunt to save the rest for the ride back home. She picked up her phone and realized she missed a text message from Sean last night. She instantly smiled and was relieved to know he actually did text her back, even though it took him a few hours. Raquel opened the text message and read it aloud.

Hey baby sorry I missed your calls. I'm in DC handling some business. Have a safe flight 2morrow, love u Ra

-Sean

I knew it had to be because of business! It had nothing to do with that bitch Keema. She nodded to herself, mentally patting herself on the back for not jumping to conclusions.

Raquel felt like she had finally won him over. She sent Sean a text telling him she couldn't wait to get back home and see him. Eager to catch her flight, Raquel headed over to the shuttle bus stop where the driver was waiting to take passengers over to the airport.

After the four minute ride, Raquel exited the shuttle and headed into the airport to handle all the preliminaries before walking to gate number A8 where she boarded the 9:15 morning flight and began to relax. All she had to do now was wait for the stewardess to take her drink order, turn on some music, and rest until she arrived in Los Angles. This would be a trip she would never forget.

***

As Sean was getting ready to leave the Aloft Hotel and make his way back to Baltimore, his phone began to vibrate. He thought it was Keema yet again but to his surprise it was Raquel. He opened up the text message.

I can't wait to get back home and see you. I love u.

-Mrs. Crosby

Sean smiled at the fact Raquel referred to herself as Mrs. Crosby. She was already thinking of herself as his wife but he knew that may not last very long. Once he broke the news about Keema being pregnant, he was almost positive Raquel would leave him.

Sean jumped into his Range Rover and headed back to Baltimore to meet up with his realtor Reuben at 9:30am. He was a short, fat, rich, Jewish man, and just the person you needed to see if you needed to make something look legit.

Reuben had all types of connections. His list included the names of judges, policeman, and shady politicians. Reuben first met Sean when he was just a little solider for Gunna. He helped them get out of a few legal situations back in the day. Before getting into the real estate business, Reuben was the best criminal lawyer in town. He was known for getting plenty of drug dealers and killers off with little to no jail time. He was also the same man who sold Sean the decoy house. And now that he needed a new place to live, Sean wouldn't think of calling on anyone else but him.

After an hour and twelve minutes of ducking and dodging through traffic, Sean pulled up to Reuben's quiet office located in what was commonly known as Jew town. This part of Park

Heights Avenue was mostly occupied by the Jewish community, hence the name.

Sean was more accustomed to being on the other side of Park Heights where all the action and commotion was. He only came to this part of the town when he needed to see Reuben, which was rare.

When he pulled up, Rueben was already standing outside eager to get started.

"Hey! My main man Sean! Always on time, how ya doing?" Reuben greeted Sean as he exited the truck.

"Hey Ben wassup? Look, I need a new place to stay ASAP. You know what I like in a place—nothing outside the city and the sooner the better." Sean quickly instructed. He had no time to waste.

"What about the house you live in now? Are you selling it?" Reuben probed Sean. He wanted to make as much money as possible but he could tell by the look Sean gave him, he was in no mood for small talk. "Never mind boss man, let's get to work. I have a few properties I can show you."

Sean followed Reuben over to the awaiting town car when suddenly his phone began to ring. He looked at the phone and it was no one other than Keema. He hit the decline button but before he could place the phone back in his pocket Keema was calling again. This time he let the phone ring until the voicemail picked up. Once the phone stopped ringing, next came a text message.

Damn. She annoying as fuck! Sean thought. He opened the text message to see what she wanted and he couldn't believe his eyes.

I know ur probably having a hard time breaking the news to your precious Raquel so I decided to help you. I texted the bitch and told her for you.

-Love, Baby Momma XOXO

Sean immediately started to panic. He had to get to the bottom of this. "Hey Reuben, sorry man, I got some shit I gotta take care of. We'll reschedule later. Here take this." Sean stuffed a thousand dollars in Reuben's hands, compensating him for his trouble. He then ran over to his Range Rover and peeled off.

Sean hit 90 miles per hour on the interstate 83 trying to make it to the house he once shared with Keema. If what she said was true then Sean was truly fucked. He pulled into a parking spot in front of the house, slammed the Rover in park and rushed to the front door. Sean used his key to enter the front door but his entry was denied.

Keema had the nerve to change the locks.

BOOM! BOOM! BOOM! BOOM! BOOM! Sean pounded on the front door, hoping Keema would answer before someone called the police.

After a few moments, Keema swung the door open screaming like a mad woman. "WHAT THE FUCK DO YOU WANT?! GET THE FUCK AWAY FROM HERE!"

Sean was never one to put his hands on a female, but when it came to Keema he thought about it a few times. He pushed Keema out the way so he could enter into the house and she began to wildly swing at him. Sean grabbed her arm stopping her before she could make contact.

"Get off me nigga!" She said struggling trying to free herself.

"Bitch, where ya fucking phone and don't make me ask you again." Sean threatened her. He needed to see the text messages in Keema's phone. He had to know if what she said was true and he wanted to see it with his own eyes. If Keema actually sent Raquel a text like she said, there was no he could save his relationship with her. He was lucky if she remained his friend.

Keema was not giving up her phone without a fight. She never thought Sean would actually treat her this way. It just got worse and worse but Keema didn't seem to understand the part she played in all this. Yes they had their differences but what couple didn't? Keema really believed Sean loved her. Even though she knew he had feelings for Raquel, Keema never thought she would lose her man to another woman.

As Keema proceeded to ignore Sean and walk up the stairs, he raced over to her, grabbed her by the throat and forced her up against the wall.

"Now I'mma ask you one more time, WHERE THE FUCK IS THE PHONE?!" Sean yelled never letting go of her throat.

Keema didn't see that coming at all. Would Sean really harm her while she was pregnant with his child? "Please... I can't breathe, the baby..." she pleaded as she tried to pry his hand from around her neck.

Sean was in such a rage he didn't care about the unborn child she was carrying. He was so fucking fed up with Keema and her drama that nothing mattered to him but HIM.

"Bitch, fuck all that. Keep playing and you'll be dead in this mothafucka! Now where is it?" Sean muttered through clenched teeth.

"It's upstairs on the dresser." Keema finally whispered with the little bit of breath she had left. Sean let go of Keema and raced upstairs to the bedroom. He found the phone on the dresser just like she said. He unlocked the phone and began to read the text messages. Not only did he discover Keema was living foul, but she had in fact texted Raquel. His heart dropped to the pit of his stomach.

I'm pregnant bitch.

-Keema XOXO

At that moment Sean knew it was over with Raquel.

He went back down the stairs to find Keema sitting on the floor crying. He walked up to her, looked Keema in the eyes and told her, "Bitch you are dead to me. Don't call me for shit."

Sean then spit directly in Keema's face and walked out the front door, never looking back.

***

Three drinks and five and a half hours later, Raquel was finally in the beautiful city of Los Angeles. It was such a relief to finally be off the plane. She loved flying above the earth, admiring the scenery but she had seen more than enough for one day. She was definitely right about the heat in LA. It was only spring but it felt like the middle of summer.

Raquel switched her shoes and removed her hoodie as she waited for her luggage to spin around the conveyor belt. She looked down at her watch which read 3:05pm. But in all actuality, it was only 12:05pm on the west coast. She had never traveled to a different time zone before and the time thing would take some getting use to. After retrieving her luggage, Raquel walked outside to find her agent Charles standing beside a limo.

She thought of the day they met. Raquel was at a photo shoot when this tall man with almond brown skin, dark mysterious eyes, and a perfectly shaped goatee approached her and asked if she needed representation. Raquel blew him off at first but after she finally called and met with him, the rest was history.

"Hey Raquel, how are you? How was the party?" He asked while walking towards Raquel to assist her with the luggage. It had been a few days since they saw each other. Charles didn't make it to her party since he was in LA preparing everything for them.

"Hey Charles it was great!" Raquel said as they quickly embraced and entered the limo that would *chauffeur* them during Raquel's stay. "So where we going?" She was excited to be in the City of Angels.

"We going over to the Fashion District, we have two meetings and both have the potential to bring in big money. Then you have a photo shoot tomorrow morning with Jacquelyn. You know—the gig you already booked because you were blessed with those beautiful eyes." Charles briefed her with a smile.

Raquel was going to be the face of a new and upcoming eyeglass company who specializes in fashion forward frames. There were already a few big name stars seen sporting the brand at red carpet events and during televised interviews.

"Well I'm ready to work!" Raquel said snapping her fingers getting into Diva mode.

Everything between them was strictly business. They both loved to hustle and together they made money and fast! Whatever the other needed, they had each other's back as long as it involved money being made in the process.

"It's only about 30-35 minutes away, but keep in mind LA has the worst fucking traffic. We are an hour ahead of schedule though. I made sure to get you here early just in case there were any delays. Here. Take this and make it quick. We gotta air out." Charles said as he handed Raquel a blunt. She admired that Charles was always on his shit, not only with the business, but he always made sure Raquel had whatever she needed; whether it was legal or not.

Raquel always smoked before a gig or meeting just to take the edge off. After smoking a little less than half of the blunt, she put it out and placed it in the ashtray. She also made sure to sanitize her hands and spray herself with perfume.

When they finally arrived in the district, Raquel was beyond nervous. This was the first time she had ever done anything of this caliber. This wasn't just an urban magazine or some music video, this was the big time.

"Okay Raquel, lemme give you the run down real quick. The client's name is Nina. She is looking for someone to represent her new line of bridal gowns. The second meeting will be a few doors down with a guy named Christophe who has a line of handbags. We'll knock out the two meetings then grab something to eat." Charles said.

"That sounds good." Raquel said taking slow deep breaths. Her legs began to shake as her nerves started to get the best of her.

"Don't be nervous, you'll be fine just be yaself, you got it. Now let's go get this paper, then we can celebrate." Charles said confidently. He believed in her a hundred percent.

As they pulled up and stepped out the limo, Raquel took one last deep breath before entering the building where they were greeted by a very peppy lady.

"Hello Ms. James. We have been looking forward to this meeting for quite some time now." The tall blonde said as she greeted them with a handshake. "And you sir must be Charles, I'm Stacey. Follow me this way! I'll walk you to the conference room where Nina should be. Oh and just to give you a heads up, Christophe is here too. Word spreads quickly in the district so they decided to do a joint meeting. Hope that's alright and you guys didn't hear it from me."

Raquel's heart skipped a beat as Stacy rambled on. She did not like the idea of a joint meeting. Not only did she have to impress them both, but at the *same* time. She looked over at Charles and saw by the expression on his face that he was not happy either.

They entered the conference room and sat at the long cherry wood conference table. "They should be right in. Would you two care for anything to drink while you wait? Water, tea, coffee, champagne?" Stacey asked.

"Water would be just fine, thank you." Charles replied.

As Stacey exited the room, Raquel questioned her agent about the double meeting.

"There's no way you knew about this and didn't tell me right?" she asked with a slight attitude.

"Now come on. You know me better than that, this ain't how we operate. Trust me, I'm pissed about it too but we gotta keep a cool head and handle business. Just focus on the meeting, I got everything else." Charles assured her.

Just as they wrapped up their private conversation, in walked Stacey with a man and woman assumed to be Christophe and Nina. Nina looked very down to earth and easy going but Christophe on the other hand looked like he could be rather difficult to impress.

"Well hello. I'm Nina and this is Christophe. I hope you don't mind the joint meeting but once we heard we both had a meeting with you, we figured this would be easier." She said matter-of-factly. Nina was very sure of herself and accustomed to calling the shots.

"Well, actually it would have been better if we were informed properly so we could prepare. It's a little off-putting to come here and be thrown into a situation when other things were spoken and agreed on. Nevertheless, shall we begin?" Charles said cool as a cucumber.

Nina sat back in her chair feeling like a school girl who was in trouble with the principal. Charles was absolutely right. Nina would have been pretty upset if someone did that to her. She wished she had been more thoughtful.

"Yes Charles, you are absolutely correct, my deepest apologies. Hopefully this won't affect our business." She said sincerely.

"Yes. We are deeply apologetic. It shall never happen again." Christophe stated in a deep French accent.

After the air was cleared, they started the meeting off without a hitch. They discussed Raquel's resume, browsed through her portfolio, and she even modeled pieces from each of the designer's lines.

Raquel was totally in her element. Nothing brought her more joy than modeling. This was her idea of heaven.

"Well I think that concludes our meeting. What do you think Christophe?" Nina asked.

"Yes I believe so." He was a man of few words.

Raquel was pretty good at reading people but she didn't know what to think of this man. She knew she had Nina in the bag but him, she wasn't so sure about.

"Stacey, can you come escort Raquel and Charles to the waiting area please? Thank you." Nina spoke over the intercom.

Within a few moments Stacey was walking in the room to take Charles and Raquel to the front.

"We will discuss a few things and get right with you guys." Nina said before closing the door.

Raquel was full of anxiety. Her hands were getting sweaty and her legs wouldn't stop shaking. She wanted to win them both over, not just one. Being the face of three popular brands would give her career the push it needed. Her face would be seen worldwide and her name would become common among all types of people.

After about fifteen minutes of waiting, Raquel could hear Nina over the intercom asking Stacey to bring them back into the conference room. As the door opened, she could see a silver platter with a bottle of Dom and four champagne glasses sitting on the table. Raquel didn't know what to think. She was offered champagne when they first arrived so maybe this didn't necessarily mean she got *either* job.

"Please come in and enjoy a glass of champagne with us. We spoke and we want to apologize again for the way we handled the meeting. It was not fair for us to force a joint meeting on you guys without warning." Nina began. "Now I assure you, even though this was a group meeting our decisions were made independently..."

Her introduction made Raquel feel like there was bad news coming. *They're buttering me up because of how they went about this fucking meeting. Not because they chose to work with me.* She wanted Nina to hurry up and get to the point. She had enough of the small talk.

"We both love your portfolio and how you look in our products and We BOTH would like to say congratulations and welcome to our teams!" Christophe finished off as he and Nina rose from their seats to end the meeting with a toast.

Raquel was in complete and utter shock! Did she hear him correctly? She was so excited that she didn't react at all.

"Come on Raquel, aren't you going to toast with us?" Charles said teasingly. He knew she was in shock, as he was too.

Raquel snapped out her daze and stood to her feet to join everyone else in the toast. "Oh my gosh,. I'm sorry you guys. I'm really.... surprised! I don't know what to say, thank you." She said teary eyed.

"Let's all just say cheers!" suggested Nina.

"CHEERS!" shouted the foursome as they clinked glasses, taking a sip of bubbly.

Raquel was looking forward to both new partnerships, she couldn't wait to get back home and share the good news with Keisha.

Chapter 4

After leaving the joint meeting, Charles instructed the driver to take them to the restaurant where he made dinner reservations. They would eat and have a celebratory drink before heading to the hotel to relax and unwind for the night. The usual seventeen minute ride took the driver about twenty nine minutes due to traffic but Raquel didn't mind it one bit. She spent the entire ride daydreaming, overjoyed by her good news. The limo driver dropped them off in front of one of Charles's favorite spots in LA, The Grill on The Alley. He advised the driver he would call for him once they were wrapping up with dinner.

Charles walked in the restaurant with Raquel, gave the name for the reservation and they were seated right away. Charles ordered the Patron Margarita for Raquel and a Hennessey on the rocks for himself. The waiter gave them a few minutes to look over the menu while he went to get their drinks.

"So how you feel about today?" Charles asked. He was satisfied with the outcome but he wanted to know her thoughts.

Raquel wasn't sure on how to put her feelings into words. She knew coming to LA would be life changing for her but she had no idea it would happen this fast. "Man, I was not expecting that at all. You saw how my ass was still seated while everyone else was toasting," Raquel said laughing at herself.

She had never been so caught off guard in her life. She hoped the rest of her career would go just as smooth.

"Yea. You did sit there like you were frozen in time. You did ya thing in there so they would be foolish to not sign you." Charles said stroking her ego. He was always fully confident in Raquel's ability, which is why he made her first priority when it came to his list of clients. He had other models that brought in decent money but it was nothing close to what Raquel pulled in.

"I really want to thank you Charles. We've worked hard this past year and its finally paying off. I really appreciate you." Raquel told him sincerely.

Charles loved listening to Raquel speak, especially when it was from the heart. There was something about the way she spoke, her voice was hypnotizing. "You are more than welcome, and every bit of the work we put in was definitely well worth it." Charles had to mentally remind himself not to get captivated by Raquel which he had to do every so often.

The waiter returned to the table with their drinks and took their order. "I'll have the Chicken Marsala with a baked potato and what will you have Charles?" Raquel asked him.

"I'll have the prime New York steak with the grilled asparagus."

As they waited for their food Charles and Raquel reviewed the contracts Stacey had given him before they left the office. If Raquel agreed to the terms they would fax them over to the lawyer for review and move on from there. As far as Raquel could see everything within the contract seemed more than fair and she was excited to move forward.

After enjoying their meals Charles called the limo driver who stated he would be around to pick them up in a few minutes. Once inside the limo all Raquel wanted to do was relax. It had been a long day and the alcohol she had been drinking throughout the day was starting to kick in. She grabbed the leftover blunt out of the ashtray and this time Charles joined in the festivities.

He thought about all the money they could possibly make together. He was working on getting Raquel booked for a big project in the Bahamas but he didn't want to mention it until he was one hundred percent sure the job was hers.

They continued to pass the blunt back and forth until it was gone. Once they arrived at the Lux City Center Hotel, the limo driver opened the door to allow Charles and Raquel to exit. Charles removed Raquel's luggage, carrying it for her as they walked into the hotel entrance, through the lobby and onto the elevator.

They rode all the way up to the tenth floor where their rooms where.

"Well here we are. Room 1014 is yours, and I'm in 1016. Our rooms are connected through this door here. They lock so don't even think about sneaking into my room." Charles said jokingly.

"Shut up, you wish!" Raquel said cracking up with laughter as she pushed him out the door. "I'll be over there once I shower so we can keep celebrating."

She was tired after a long day but this was a moment she wanted to remember. So Raquel took a shower, put on her bra, along with some basketball shorts and a wife beater. Since she was going next door with Charles the usual birthday suit and robe wasn't the most appropriate outfit.

It was then Raquel realized she had been so busy all day that she hadn't talked to or texted Sean all day. She wasn't even sure if he called her, or if anyone else had for that matter. She reached into her purse and pulled out her phone but it was dead.

Raquel placed the phone on the charger while she pulled some things out of her luggage for tomorrow. Once her phone powered on, it beeped a few times letting her know she had some messages. To her surprise not one of them was from Sean.

"Maybe he was waiting for me. He knew I would be busy today." Raquel reasoned with herself. She saw a text from Brenda and a number she wasn't familiar with. She opened the text and what she read blew her mind.

I'm pregnant bitch.

- Keema XOXO

Her eyes instantly became filled with hot steamy tears that poured down her cheeks. It all made sense to her now. It had never been this hard to get in touch with Sean, ever! Since he left her house the other morning to supposedly break it off with Keema, he had been ignoring Raquel's every attempt to contact her.

That taking care of business shit was nothing but a lie and a distraction from the real issue. She thought bitterly. Raquel didn't know what to do. She really did love Sean, she always had, and now she opened herself up only to be hurt. She knew she had to break it off with him ASAP. She didn't even want to see him for the time being. Raquel didn't know if she could ever forgive him. She decided she wasn't going to call Sean. She would just simply text him and end things that way.

I heard the news congratulations, we are done.

-Fuck You

Raquel couldn't get a hold of her emotions. She had to pull herself together for tomorrow but her heart was broken. She couldn't believe Sean. She thought they were better than this. They trusted each other with everything, even their very own lives.

Even though it was wrong, Raquel wished she had beaten that baby right out of Keema's stomach the other night. And maybe if Sean hadn't pulled her off of Keema it was a strong possibility she would have.

KNOCK! KNOCK!

"You okay?" Charles shouted through the closed door. He could overhear her crying and wanted to check on her.

"Hold on. I'll come over in a minute." Raquel said sounding muffled. She walked into the bathroom to wash her face before going over to talk to Charles. She pulled herself together and joined him in his suite.

Charles had never seen Raquel this upset before, he was a bit concerned. "What's going on lil' mama? You know you can talk to me. Wassup?" Charles asked as he poured Raquel a double shot of Patron.

Raquel took the shot back slamming the glass on the table. "Nothing, I just trusted the wrong person that's all."

Charles could tell this was about a man. He knew woman pretty well. He walked over to his stash so he could roll them a blunt. He knew it may be a long night. "You wanna talk about it?"

Even though Raquel wanted and needed to talk, she didn't want to ruin the mood. After all, they were supposed to be celebrating Raquel's success.

"Naw, I'm good. Thanks." Raquel whispered softly.

Charles hoped whatever it was wouldn't ruin the rest of the trip; they still had business to attend to. "Come on crybaby, let's go outside." he teased.

The crybaby comment made Raquel laugh; she was not one to shed tears often. She let Sean take her out of character but she couldn't help it. They sat outside on the semi-private balcony and began to smoke, passing the blunt back and forth.

Charles wanted Raquel to talk, not only so she could feel better but he also wanted her mind right for the photo shoot. He understood something was hurting her but that couldn't stop the money flow.

After a few minutes of silence Raquel began to open up. "I made the mistake of trusting a friend with my heart and it ended up being the biggest mistake of my life. I don't think I wanna see or talk to him ever again." She confessed holding back tears.

Charles knew how dramatic women could be so he wasn't sure if it was something significant or if she was overreacting. "What do you mean? Was it that bad?" He questioned, trying to get a better idea of the situation.

"Yeah It's that bad. He's having a baby and I found out from his bitch and not him. I haven't even heard from him. I thought we had a future... How fucking stupid of me." Raquel said, feeling sorry for herself.

Charles felt bad for her as well. She was a good woman and he didn't believe she deserved that, no woman did. "Wow... So he cheated on you and got another broad pregnant? That's wild!" He said, never imagining himself in a predicament like that.

"Well... no, he didn't cheat. We weren't together. It's... a lil' complicated." Raquel tired explaining.

Charles was completely confused. How could she be upset about a nigga who wasn't her man having a baby? "So ya'll not a couple but you upset that he's having a baby and didn't tell you?" He shook his head. "Sorry, ma, but it sounds like you mad because somebody beat you to the punch." He told Raquel with all honesty.

That particular statement pissed Raquel off. He didn't know the full story and she felt like he was judging her. Charles could see the anger on her face. You could always tell how Raquel was feeling just by looking at her.

"Chill, don't get upset. I'm just keeping it real."

Raquel snatched the blunt out his hand and began to smoke. He laughed and threw his hands in the air letting her know he didn't want any beef. He knew she could cut a nigga with her words and he didn't want any parts of it.

"Yes he's in a relationship with her but the other night we confessed our love for one another and we decided to be together. He said he would break it off with her. Then I'm calling and texting and getting nothing." Raquel rattled off as her eyes started to tear up again.

Charles hated to see a woman cry. He saw his mom cry a lot as a child. He wiped her eyes and took the blunt from her to offer some advice. "Don't cry ma but listen, you put yaself in this position. You chose to fuck with a man that was already taken. You say y'all decided to be together a few days ago but how far along is shorty? Did he know already chick was pregnant?"

Raquel sat silently thinking about what Charles said as she looked out over the balcony. He had a point. Even though Sean was wrong for not telling her, she knew Keema was his woman. Anything that happened prior to her coming in the picture had nothing to do with her, but she still didn't want to deal with Sean for the moment.

It was still wrong for him to ignore me and hide the truth, Raquel thought. "Yeah you have a point." She finally spoke.

Her mind was spinning as they sat outside for a while longer after their conversation. By this point Raquel had three double shots of Patron and she was a bit past tipsy. She started to walk over to the edge of the balcony to get a better view but she stumbled.

"Whoa. You good?" Charles asked as he caught Raquel.

They locked eyes as Charles still had his arms wrapped around Raquel from breaking her drunken fall. She never realized how handsome Charles was until now as she looked up at him.

Raquel leaned forward and unexpectedly kissed Charles. They briefly shared a nice sensual kiss until Charles abruptly stopped the unsuspected moment of passion.

"Yo, what you doing?!" he asked backing up from Raquel. It wasn't that he wasn't attracted to her, Charles actually had a thing for Raquel but he promised himself before deciding to work with her that he would *never* involve himself with Raquel on a personal level. His money was more important than any woman and her current situation proved how things could go wrong.

Raquel had done it again. It was something with her and Patron that made her do stupid shit. *First I made a move on Sean and now Charles.*

"Fuck! I'm sorry Charles. I didn't mean to do that. Um… I gotta go get ready for tomorrow. I'll see you in the morning." She lied as she ran back into her half of the suite locking the adjoining door behind her.

***

Sean was back at The Aloft Hotel pacing back and forth as he tried to make sense of everything going on around him. He didn't know what to do but he knew he had to come up with a plan and fast. Sean wanted to explain everything to Raquel but what would he say?

As he continued to gather his thoughts, his phone began to vibrate on the table. He picked up the phone and saw a text message from his love Raquel. His heart started beating like a drum. He knew that if she looked at her phone, more than likely she saw the message from Keema. Sean didn't know what to expect but he knew it couldn't be anything good. He opened the text and was instantly angered by what he read.

I heard the news congratulations, we are done.

-Fuck You

Sean immediately called Raquel's phone and was directed to the voicemail. He tried repeatedly but it was the same thing each time. He could tell that Raquel was pushing the decline button so he decided to text her.

Answer the phone Ra, we need to talk.

- Sean

He didn't expect an answer, he knew how stubborn Raquel was but to his surprise his phone buzzed instantly with a response.

It's too late and my name is Raquel.

-Not Ra

Sean was enraged. He and Raquel never had any big argument where they didn't speak to each other. They had their little spats here and there but never anything like this. He grabbed his keys and headed back out the door. He was going to pay Keema another visit.

***

Back home in Baltimore, Keisha couldn't take it anymore. She needed to talk to her best friend. She had been walking on eggshells ever since her beating from Dre and she was more than ready to leave him. She was tired of being terrified by her new husband. Keisha never knew when or if he would hit her. For Dre it was a game, he liked to taunt her. He would threaten her, throw things just barely missing, or ball his fist up bucking at her as if he was going to punch her.

Since the day they returned home from their honeymoon, he started to become the old abusive Dre she knew from before. Keisha felt beyond stupid. Not only did she take him back after he kicked their unborn child out her stomach, but she also married him. And she was disgusted with herself.

Keisha picked up her cell phone and tried to call her friend but to her surprise there was no answer. Raquel always answered the phone for her, but since she was away on business, Keisha figured maybe she was busy so she texted instead of calling a second time.

We need to talk. I need your help.

-Love Keish

She sent the text and quickly deleted it just in case Dre walked in the room. He knew the passcode to her phone and he would know something was up seeing that text message. In the meantime Keisha would just play her cards right. She knew once her ride or die came back in town she would help her come up with a plan.

***

Raquel continued to lie in the bed as she tried to pull herself together. She repeatedly hit the ignore button on her cell as Sean continued to call back to back. She was in no mood to speak to him, plus she had to think about how she was going to face her agent after she kissed him. She'd never had any romantic thoughts about Charles until now. He was very handsome, maybe more attractive than Sean, but she was not about to ruin her business like she did her friendship.

Raquel's thoughts were interrupted by the sound of her phone vibrating once again. She just knew it was Sean, but when she looked at the phone it was her bestie Keisha. Seeing her friend's name appear on the screen made her crack a smile. She knew Keisha would always have her back if nobody else did. She opened the text message sent by her friend.

We need to talk. I need your help.

-Love Keish

"Lord, what does she want now?!" Raquel asked herself. Keisha was her girl and all but she always wanted something. Still, she knew if the roles were reversed Keisha would help her out too. Raquel was not in the mood to talk to anyone right now so she texted her friend back instead of calling.

I need to talk to you too. See you when I get home tomorrow.

-Your bestie bitch

Raquel giggled after typing her text. She loved her best friend to the core. Their bond was unbreakable. Even though Sean had let her down she knew Keisha was always the one person she could still trust.

Raquel decided to speak to Charles before she went to bed. After all, she had to see him in the morning so why not clear the air now? She walked over the connecting door and knocked, waiting for Charles to answer. After a few seconds the door swung open and there he stood.

Damn he looks good without a shirt, Raquel thought, fighting to stay focused on the issue at hand.

"Can I come in?" She asked looking like a lost child.

"Come on girl, stop tripping." Charles said as he walked back over to the sofa where he was watching ESPN and enjoying a glass of Hennessey.

Raquel slowly entered the room and walked towards Charles but stopped in the middle of the floor. She had no idea what she was going to say to him, but she knew she had to say something, "Charles, listen. I'm sorry for what happened earlier. I don't know what I was thinking. Lately it seems like liquor is bringing out another side of me. I'm a lil' embarrassed."

Charles had actually enjoyed the kiss, a lot more than she thought. "It's cool, nothing to be sorry for. We all have our moments. Here, relax." He suggested as he stood up and walked over to Raquel who was still standing in the middle of the hotel suite. He handed Raquel his glass and stood there watching her enjoy the cognac.

Charles had been doing some thinking of his own while Raquel was next door. He had something he wanted to ask to her. "Yo, can I ask you a question?"

She shook her head 'yes' as she continued to enjoy the much needed drink.

"Can I have my moment now?" Charles asked as he took a step closer to her.

Raquel felt like a deer in headlights. There was no way this could be happening. It was like déjà vu. Before she could process the question and give an answer, Charles softly grabbed Raquel's face and kissed her. She surprised herself when she kissed him back throwing caution to the wind. Every worry Raquel had at that moment escaped her as her body began to melt.

As they continued to kiss, Charles slowly began to slide his hand up Raquel's thigh, and underneath her shorts. He then eased two fingers into her sweet spot and Raquel gasped for air as she felt Charles' thick manly fingers inside of her. He continued to move his fingers in and out of her, rotating them from left to right.

Raquel began to moan as Charles played with her kitty. She closed her eyes and envisioned them making love. He continued to please her as her wetness covered his fingers. He was harder than a rock and he wanted to fuck Raquel so bad, but there was more to it than that for him. He decided he wanted Raquel to be his woman, so he resisted the urge and focused on pleasing her.

Within minutes Raquel was cumming all over his fingers while holding back screams of passion. She didn't want Charles to know how much she was enjoying herself, although it was quite obvious.

Charles slowly pulled out his fingers and sucked all of her juices off of them. "Mmm... You taste good." Charles looked Raquel dead in her eyes.

She didn't know what to do. She thought about riding him right there on the floor after she looked down and saw a massive bulge in his pants. Raquel knew she couldn't take it there with Charles though, not after everything that happened with Sean.

"What was that, Charles? We can't do this, this is crazy!" Raquel said, making her way towards the sofa to put some space between them.

"Look I never wanted to push up on you or nothing like that—I mean, you bad as fuck but we *do* work together. I told myself you were off limits but fuck that, I want you." Charles stated, sitting next to her on the sofa so he could further express himself. "I want to take care of you, business wise and personally. I see something in you, and I want to explore it. I been watching you for a minute trying to resist the urge but after you kissed me I couldn't fight it. No rush but at the end of the day, you gonna be mine." he told her confidently.

Raquel was in shock. This was Sean all over again. *Damn Raquel why did you have to go and kiss this man? I'm not going to make the same mistake twice.* She thought.

"I don't know, Charles. This is a bad idea. You see what I'm dealing with now. I don't want nothing to do with Sean and I don't want us to ever get to that point. That could potentially stop our money flow." She reasoned.

Charles knew this wasn't going to be easy but he never gave up on anything he wanted without a fight. "I hear you ma, but the offer is there. You know I'm a single man and I will continue to be until you're my woman." Charles said as he kissed Raquel's hand.

His lips were so full and soft. Raquel wondered how they would feel on her second set of lips which were dying for some more attention after he finished finger fucking her. One part of Raquel was telling her to go for it and the other half was saying run for your life!

For now Raquel decided she was going to focus on her money and nothing else, even though her pussy told her something different.

"I just don't see this turning out well and I don't believe in fairy tales either. Thanks for making things less awkward between us." Raquel joked as she stood up, kissed Charles on the forehead and exited his half of the room.

Chapter 5

The next morning Raquel was beyond tired after last night's episode, but she had one more task to complete. She rolled out the bed, quickly showered, and made her way downstairs to meet Charles with luggage in hand. After the photo shoot with Jacquelyn, Raquel would go straight to the airport and fly back to Baltimore. LA was beautiful and the weather was spectacular but she was ready to go back home.

Once Raquel arrived, everything moved at the speed of light. As she and Charles exited the limo, they were greeted by Jacquelyn, the creator of the line. She was a tall, skinny, black woman who wore glasses that Raquel assumed where from her collection. She also had great fashion sense.

"Hey doll, glad you made it here safely! It's nice to see you again, you too Charles." Jacquelyn said as she kissed their cheeks. Things will move rather quickly so I hope you're ready." Jacquelyn informed her as they walked inside.

The glam squad wasted no time getting Raquel prepared. One minute Raquel was in hair and makeup and the next she was being zipped into a long beautiful, form fitting gown that complemented her figure very well. She slipped on her shoes and was rushed on set. Just as Raquel started to enter her zone, smiling and posing in front of the camera, the next thing she knew boom! The shoot was finished.

"Alright! I think we got it people!" shouted the photographer.

Raquel wasn't so sure. She was just beginning to warm up. She had never done a photo shoot so quickly before. She knew for her next shoot she needed to start off strong right away, there was no time to waste once in front of the photographer.

"Wow! Raquel, you did great! Once we go over the images with our team we will have a meeting with you via video chat. You will choose three photos out of five. Out of those three we will choose one for a billboard and the other two will be used for the store displays." Jacquelyn informed as she walked Charles and Raquel outside to the limo.

Raquel was ecstatic to hear Jacquelyn thought she did so well. She also couldn't believe her face would be on a billboard in LA. "Thank you so much Jacquelyn! I hope to see you again soon." She said as the two women hugged one another.

"Next time you come back you have to stay for a little while so I can show you around. See ya!" Jacquelyn said waving goodbye as she walked back into the building.

Inside the limo Charles just stared at Raquel admiring the hard working woman she was. Being a model wasn't as easy as everyone thought. It took a lot of hard work and dedication and Raquel was taking the industry by storm.

Charles was serious about seeing where things could go between them. He had a nice big house and no one to share it with. Charles came close to being married once before, that was until he discovered his ex-fiancé was having an affair with one of the rappers he previously worked with. Charles put some of his other models in a music video and his scheming ex used one of the video vixens to get closer to the artist. Once he found out about the affair, he called the engagement off and has been single ever since.

Charles always pictured himself being married and having a family. He was raised in a household with both his parents. They were married forty seven years before his father's passing a few years back. He wanted to do things a little differently from his father though. He watched his father mistreat his mother a lot of the time. He was never physical with her but he would cheat on his mother and not be discreet about it.

His parents were from the old school so his mom did not believe in getting a divorce. She stuck by her husband during those rough times and although his dad eventually changed his ways, Charles wanted to right by his woman from the start. He didn't want his love to hurt the way his mother had for so many years. He vowed to be a good husband if he ever got married.

He had taken Raquel around plenty of rappers, athletes, movie stars, etc., but she never sweated them; even though a few of them offered her everything but the world itself. He could see money didn't move her and that turned him on. She was self-sufficient and took very good care of herself.

"Damn nigga what you looking at?" Raquel asked jokingly realizing Charles was eyeing her.

"My future wife." Charles smoothly answered without hesitation.

Raquel just sat back shaking her head. She did not want to give into temptation but it was getting harder by the day. The more she thought about it, the more she was interested. She never saw Charles with a bunch of woman or hanging out in the strip clubs. He was always about his money and nothing else. Not to mention he treated his mother like a queen and to Raquel that meant he would do the same for his lady.

They also had good times together but it was never on a romantic level. It was getting harder not to think about entertaining the idea after their business trip took a small detour. On the other hand Raquel was just getting a taste of fame and fortune and she didn't want to complicate things by fucking her agent. She just sat in silence looking out the window as they continued to the airport.

As they pulled up to LAX, Raquel began to gather her things and prepared to exit the limo.

Charles slid closer to Raquel, looking her straight in the eye, "Don't forget what I said, even if ya answer is no then I'll respect that, no hard feelings. But if you wit it I promise you, even if we don't last forever, it won't be no bad blood between us. I won't hurt you ma, I'm a one woman type of dude." Charles spoke from the heart.

Raquel was starting to develop a soft spot for Charles. He was sweet and charming, *and* fine as fuck.

She responded by gently stroking Charles' face and kissed him on the cheek, "Come on before we miss this flight, boy." Raquel exited the limo, and they entered the airport together.

***

Sean raced down I-295 as he headed to Keema's place. He was going through all this bullshit and he didn't even know if the girl was really pregnant!

"Bitch talking bout she pregnant! When the fuck was she gonna tell me and how fucking long has she known?" Sean mumbled aloud as he sped down the highway.

He was going to take Keema to the hospital and see what was really going on. He was hoping it was all a lie just to try to keep him in her life. Whatever was going on today would be the day he would find out the truth. Sean figured more than likely Keema was home since he took the keys to the car he bought her.

There was barely any traffic so Sean made it in town within an hour. He walked up to the door and called Keema's cell phone for her to unlock it.

"Hello?" Keema answered sounding sluggish.

"Get up and open the door." He ordered.

Within moments Keema was opening the door to let Sean in. She was dressed in a white robe and bedroom slippers. She looked as if she had been lying around all day.

"Go put some clothes on we got somewhere to go. You got five minutes. I'll be in the car," Sean demanded, shutting the door behind him.

A few minutes later, Keema walked out the front door and got into the passenger seat.

"Where we going?" she asked a bit confused. He was the last person she expected to be taking her anywhere.

"Johns Hopkins," Sean coldly replied.

Keema sat back in her seat and remained quiet for the remainder of the short ride. She didn't know what to think. Sean had become a different person over the past few days and Keema was beginning to fear Sean. He had never been so cruel to her, and she fucked up a lot of times before. But maybe this time she had gone overboard.

As they got closer and closer to the hospital Keema began to get antsy. Sean turned onto Orleans St. and proceeded to the emergency room entrance. He jumped out, throwing his keys to the valet attendant as he walked around the other side, opening the door for Keema so he could escort her to the front desk.

"Just go along with what I say. I need to know what the fuck is going on. Don't say nothing stupid." Sean warned.

"How can I help you?" the young girl behind the desk asked.

"This is my girlfriend Takeema Grantley. She just found out she's pregnant but she's been having some pains and cramps in her stomach. We need to see a doctor," he lied.

Sean knew that coming to the hospital was the fastest way to find out if Keema was actually pregnant or not. It was the weekend and the doctor offices were closed, plus, a same day appointment was unlikely anyway. Sean hoped he would be able to tell Raquel it was all a lie when she returned home. *This bitch has to be lying*, he thought.

"Ok, ma'am. Fill out these forms and bring them back when you're finished."

Keema snatched the clipboard from the young woman and walked over to the waiting area with Sean.

"What are you doing, why are we here?" she asked curiously as she took a seat beside him. Keema decided to press her luck since they were at the hospital. It was unlikely he would try to hurt her here unless he wanted to be in the bookings.

Sean was not in the mood to explain shit to this woman but he had to play it cool so she would go along with it. "Look, yo. You claim you pregnant, you ruined my fucking house, *and* you told Raquel so you owe me. If you ain't got nothing to hide you'll shut the fuck up and fill out them papers so we can see the doctor."

Keema was a little nervous, she hated doctors and hospitals but she had to go along with what Sean said or he would suspect something was up. "Ok nigga. Whateva. You ain't got shit better to do than sit up in the fucking hospital. It's four in the afternoon. We gonna be here all fucking night," she mumbled under her breath.

After filling out the paperwork, she handed it back with an attitude. Keema was given an ID bracelet and told to have a seat.

I hope I won't have to wait long, she thought impatiently. After all she was a pregnant woman complaining of cramps.

After about an hour and forty five minutes of waiting, a middle aged woman dressed in multi-colored scrubs called her name, "Ms. Takeema Grantley."

Both Keema and Sean followed the woman back to a room where there was a hospital bed, two chairs, and some medical equipment. Keema was starting to get nervous all over again. She was trying to keep her composure but she couldn't help it.

"Here you go, ma'am. Put on this gown, please. You can keep on everything, just remove your shirt. The doctor will want to do an ultrasound. My name is Linda you can push that little red button if you need anything," Linda instructed while taking Keema's blood pressure, pulse, and temperature. "All your vitals are normal and the doctor will be in shortly, Ms. Grantley."

After about another twenty five minutes of sitting in silence, in walked the doctor.

"Hello. My name is Dr. Conner and I will be taking care of you today. I hear you are having some complications with your pregnancy, is that correct?" The tall, skinny, balding white doctor asked.

Keema looked at him strangely. She didn't like this whole hospital thing. She simply sat there in a daze not knowing how to answer the question.

"Yes doctor, she's been complaining of cramps." Sean spoke up. "She just recently found out she was pregnant from a home test. We haven't seen a doctor yet."

Dr. Conner looked at Keema for confirmation. Something about this seemed strange to him.

Keema halfway smiled and shook her head in agreement.

"Ok then. I will have someone take you for an ultrasound. We can take a look, see what's going on and you can have your first pictures of the baby to take home with you," Dr. Conner informed before disappearing out the room.

Sean's leg began to shake nervously. It was all starting to feel very real to him. Even though he thought Keema was lying about the whole thing, if she was telling the truth he would become a father in just a few short months, and he and Keema weren't even together. He never wanted to have a child by a woman he couldn't be with. Sean wanted a family, not a child and baby momma.

After a few minutes, Linda returned with a wheelchair to take Keema to radiology. She could see the worry on Keema's face as she approached her. "Oh don't worry honey, it's just hospital policy," she said soothingly. "You can come along if you would like sir."

Keema sat in the wheelchair and Sean followed behind them as they made their way to what felt like death row. Once they arrived, Sean and Keema sat and waited for the technician to bring them inside the room to complete the test.

Sean's mind was running wild. His whole life was resting on this one moment. Not only was he worried about losing Raquel, but the bigger issue at hand was his life could change forever. He would have a person he was responsible for, someone who would depend on him. What if it was a boy? He didn't want his son in the street life, and he wouldn't want his daughter dating a hustler either. He wasn't ready for this at all.

"Yo. If it's something you need to tell me, say it now," Sean said breaking the silence. Keema wasn't sure what he meant by that. She was just starting to relax a little then Sean rattled her nerves all over again. She didn't answer him, she just sat there silently.

The technician walked out and wheeled Keema into the room as Sean followed. The tech instructed Keema to lie on the table and lift up her gown, exposing only her abdomen, keeping the breast covered. In a few short moments the truth would be out and Sean was nervous as hell.

He did notice a slight pudge in Keema's belly, but he figured it was just from overeating and too much beer, not pregnancy. The technician rolled the machine over to the table where Keema was laying and squeezed some cold jelly on her stomach. He moved the probe back and forth across her lower abdomen and what Sean saw stunned him.

"Here you go, ma'am. There's your baby who is about eleven weeks old. You'll be able to find out the sex in a couple more weeks," the technician informed.

Sean was in disbelief, the bitch really was pregnant!

Keema didn't know what to think. She already knew she was pregnant but seeing the little developing baby on the screen made it all too real. She could tell by the look on Sean's face that he was in shock; she was in a little bit of shock herself. She didn't know what was going through Sean's mind. Keema was just hoping he would drop her off and leave. She didn't want to be asked any questions. She just wanted to be left alone.

I wish I hadn't said anything at all, she thought bitterly. The truth was she planned on getting an abortion anyway, but not before winning Sean back.

The five minute ride back to Keema's house seemed to take forever and there was nothing but silence. Sean didn't even have any music playing.

There were so many different things going through his mind and for once in his life he was at a loss. He didn't know what his next move would be. Sean wasn't even a hundred percent sure if Keema was keeping the baby or not, but even being in this predicament was too much to handle.

Keema tried talking to Sean a few times but he was just simply ignored her. Once he dropped her off, he started to make his way back to the hotel but suddenly decided to change his plans. He needed somewhere he could go and get his head straight and he knew just the perfect place. So Sean took the next exit off the interstate and hopped back on going back towards Baltimore.

***

When Raquel's plane finally landed she was more than relived. Her trip to LA was a little exhausting. There were a lot of high points during the trip but there was also a lot of drama. Between the bullshit with Sean and Keema, and the situation with Charles, Raquel just wanted to go home and relax. After exiting the plane and claiming her luggage, Raquel went outside to wait for the shuttle to take her back to the garage.

Once Raquel got back to her car, she loaded the bags in the trunk and started it up. She sat there smoking with the car's defrost on, trying to unwind before she started her journey home. She decided she wouldn't tell anyone she was back yet, especially Sean.

Her ride was a calm and peaceful one. She just enjoyed the familiar surroundings, feeling as though she had been gone for weeks. Raquel exited off 795 onto Owing Mill Boulevard and continued her short drive home. She parked the car in the garage and entered the house, leaving her luggage behind. She walked into her home and what she saw infuriated her.

There was Sean standing right in front of her. She was not prepared for this at all.

"What the fuck are you doing here? Get out!" Raquel screamed. She knew he had keys to her house but she never expected him to actually be there when she got home. *What the hell is he thinking? This nigga has some nerve!*

Raquel walked right past Sean and upstairs to her bedroom. She was not at all interested in talking to him. All she wanted to do was shower and relax; she also needed to talk to Keisha. She planned on waiting but after finding Sean in her house, she really needed to vent to her friend no matter how tired she was.

When they left LA it was one pm but after the flight distance and time zone change, it was nearly nine o'clock at night back home. She wasn't used to the time adjustment at all.

Raquel went into the bathroom to turn the shower water on when she heard Sean walking up the stairs. She quickly shut and locked the door in order to keep him out.

"Come on Ra, don't be like that open the door. We need to talk. Please yo," Sean pleaded.

Raquel did not care what Sean had to say. Anything he had to say, he should have told her days ago. She hated being played or lied to and Sean did both.

"Why you still here? I told you to leave. I don't care about shit you have to say," Raquel said through the closed door as she undressed and continued into the shower. She was hoping by the time she was finished Sean would have gotten the message and left.

Raquel was famous for taking unnecessarily long showers and she made sure to take extra time bathing, hoping Sean's patience would wear thin. Unfortunately, she exited the steam filled bathroom to find Sean sitting on the bed waiting for her to come out. Raquel simply rolled her eyes and walked into her closet to find something to throw on. She was going to pay her friend Keisha a surprise visit.

"Look, don't act like you don't see me sitting here. I'm trying to talk to you," Sean said getting aggravated.

Raquel continued to ignore him, pulling a pair of leggings, t-shirt, and jean jacket from her closet.

Sean was starting to get impatient. He understood why she was upset but he wanted the opportunity to explain himself and come clean on his own. He got up, snatched the clothes out of Raquel's hand, and threw them across the room. In return, Raquel backhanded Sean as hard as she could. She was fed the fuck up with him and she was not about to deal with any more of his foolishness.

"Damn yo, that's how you feel?!" Sean said rubbing his cheek. He wasn't angry and he would never think of hitting

Raquel. She was different than Keema. He never wanted to harm Keema either but she provoked him, and he just simply reacted.

"Yo, get the fuck out before you piss me off," Raquel warned. She was furious but Sean still wasn't ready to leave yet. He wanted to try and repair their relationship as well as their friendship. He just stood there looking at Raquel, realizing he may actually lose her. The longer Sean was in her presence, the angrier Raquel became.

"You could have told me the truth, but you didn't. You chose to lie, then on top of that I find out from Keema? How that bitch get my fucking phone number anyway?! You know what I don't have time for this shit. Go be wit that corny bitch! Fuck outta here!" Raquel said pushing Sean towards the bedroom door.

Sean could see how hurt and upset she was so he thought he would try and calm her down, he had to make things right. He turned around and grabbed Raquel, bear hugging her just like he did at the club.

"GET THE FUCK OFF!" she squealed, trying to escape his grip. Once out of Sean's grasp Raquel ran into the closet and got her .45 and pointed it directly at him.

"Yo what the fuck you doing?" Sean asked, backing up towards the door. He knew Raquel was pissed but he never imagined she would pull a gun out on him, especially one he bought for her.

"I'mma say this one more time, GET THE FUCK OUT!" Raquel screamed walking closer to Sean, gun aimed dead at him.

"Alright yo chill, I'm gone. That's fucked up though. You gonna pull a gun on me?" Sean was in disbelief as he walked out, never turning his back just in case Raquel left her mind back in LA and actually shot him. He decided he would give Raquel some time to cool off and try his luck again later. He wasn't ready to give up on her just yet.

Chapter 6

Raquel was beyond pissed after the stunt Sean just pulled. She could not believe how their friendship took a turn for the worst. She really needed to talk to Keisha so she put the gun back in the closet, threw on her clothes and left out the door.

Raquel made it to her friend's house within twenty minutes. She wasted no time on the beltway, doing well over the speed limit. She parked the BMW and went up to Keisha's house and rang the doorbell.

After a minute or two there wasn't an answer so she rung the bell again. She knew Keisha was home because her car was parked outside. A few more moments later, the door finally swung open and there was Dre standing there as if he wasn't going to invite her in.

Raquel always thought it was something with this dude, she just didn't know what. "Is Keish here?" she asked with a slight attitude.

Dre stood there for a moment before answering, looking Raquel up and down. "Yea she here, she upstairs," he said licking his lips.

Raquel ignored Dre, pushing past him going up the stairs to Dre's and Keisha's bedroom.

"Knock knock!" Raquel said as she opened Keisha's bedroom door.

Keisha was shocked but also relieved to see her friend. So much had been going on the last few days. "Oh shit bitch, when you get back?!" she asked, rushing over to her friend to give her a welcome home hug. Keisha was glad the swelling on her face was gone since Raquel snuck in on her.

The two embraced glad to see one another, they both had so much to tell.

"So wassup? You said you wanted to talk?" Keisha asked her friend. She wanted to hear what Raquel had to say before she dropped the biggest bomb ever on her. She didn't even know what she was going to say to Raquel. She had been hiding everything for so long and there was no way this would be easy.

"Girl, you will not believe what happened… So much fucking drama," Raquel started, shaking her head. She took a long deep breath before beginning her story. "So after Mo's the other night, I went home and tried to call Sean because I didn't hear from him all day, and I didn't get an answer. He ignored me all day, and then he sent me a text message hours and hours later saying he was busy but come to find out it was all a lie."

Raquel was getting upset just thinking of how things went down. She paused for a moment before telling Keisha the really fucked up part. She wasn't sure how her friend would react but she knew for she was would have something to say.

Keisha sat on the bed across from her best friend listening to everything she said.

"Girl, come to find out after all that bullshit he talked about us being together, Keema is pregnant with his baby. Can you believe that?!" Raquel asked her friend, looking for her input.

All Keisha did was shake her head in silence. She wasn't prepared for that bit of information at all. Instead of jumping off the bed yelling and screaming obscenities like usual, Keisha sat there absolutely dumbfounded. With everything that happened since Raquel told her about her and Sean, Keisha forgot about the whole baby situation. She never got the opportunity to ask Dre the details because he whupped her ass as soon as she walked in the door.

"Umm... did you hear me whore?! I said Keema is PREGNANT!!" Raquel reiterated, leaning in closer to her friend to make sure she got the message.

Right away Raquel knew something was up. Keisha was the type who always had an opinion, especially if it had something to do with a man. There was an awkward silence as they both sat there looking at each other, and then it hit Raquel like a ton of bricks.

She just remembered that Keisha told her a few weeks before they got married, that Dre and Keema were cousins! Raquel wasn't sure if Keisha knew about the pregnancy but her gut was saying she did because of how strange she was acting.

Before either of them could say anything, Dre burst through the bedroom door. He had been eavesdropping on their conversation the entire time. He was trying to make sure Keisha didn't tell Raquel about their altercation the other day.

They both jumped, startled by Dre's entrance. Raquel huffed and puffed, annoyed that Dre was interrupting their conversation. *What the fuck did he want anyway?*

"Raquel, what you in here yelling about Keema being pregnant for? You don't like that girl and Keisha already know, you late," Dre revealed.

He was not aware that Raquel and Sean had a thing going on. After all, it did happen overnight. Either way he wouldn't have cared. He still would have put his two cents in regardless.

Raquel's jaw dropped to the floor. She couldn't believe what this fool just said out of his mouth. She looked at Keisha with disgust on her face.

"Oh ya best friend right here ain't tell you? Hold up. Why ya nigga Sean ain't tell you? He ain't ask you to be the godmother?" Dre kept going on and on adding fuel to the fire.

"Yo, can you give us a minute?" Raquel snapped at Dre. He turned around and walked out the room, this time going downstairs. He knew that with the bit of information he just dropped they wouldn't be talking about him so he didn't feel the need to listen anymore.

Keisha was caught. Her friend not only knew that Keema was pregnant, but thanks to Dre, Raquel also knew that Keisha knew about the baby and didn't tell her.

As soon as Dre shut the door Raquel wasted no time going in on her so called friend. "So bitch you knew? At Mo's, you knew and didn't fucking say nothing?" She stood up furious about what she'd just learned.

Keisha was hoping she would have the opportunity to tell her friend before she found out, but she wasn't quick enough. "Look let me explain, Ra, I knew but..."

And before she could finish her sentence, Raquel cut her off. "BUT NOTHING! You knew and you didn't tell me. You fucking foul bitch! I thought we was better than that. What the fuck type of friend is you? You supposed to be like my big sister and look out for me and this is what you do?" She looked at Keisha with a mixture of anger and disappointment.

Raquel couldn't for the life of her understand why Keisha wouldn't tell her something this big. She would never hold important information from Keisha especially if it had something to do with her man.

"Yea I knew," Keisha began quietly, "but I wasn't sure if it was true. When Dre first told me I brushed that shit off. Then once you said you and Sean was fucking around, I wanted to get the details but I just had a lot going on these past few days. That's why I said I wanted to talk to you." She tried explaining.

Raquel was furious and what Keisha was saying right now didn't fucking matter. Not only did she feel betrayed by Sean but now she also felt betrayed by her closest friend. She was starting to feel like everyone had more loyalty to Keema than they had to her.

Raquel felt like she had no one left to turn to. She wasn't going to stay around for this bullshit. She grabbed her purse and keys, ready to storm out the house. Keisha was trying to stop her friend from leaving but once Raquel was upset it was hard to calm her down. She was the type that needed a moment to recoup before she would hear anything you had to say.

Keisha ran over to Raquel and grabbed her arm, trying to get her to stay and talk things out.

"Bitch, get the fuck off me! You lucky you my nigga or else I would beat the fuck out you," Raquel said snatching her arm away and proceeded to leave the house.

Raquel hopped back in her BMW and peeled off with no destination in mind. As she raced up the street her phone began to ring. She answered the phone not looking at the screen expecting it to be Keisha.

"Bitch, I don't have no I rap for you right now!" Raquel yelled into the receiver.

"Well damn, what did do?" the male voice on the other end asked.

Raquel didn't catch the voice right away, but when she looked at the phone it said Money. It was the name she stored Charles' number under.

"Oh my bad Charles. I thought you were someone else. Wassup?" she asked him calming herself down.

"I was just calling to check on you, see if you made it in safe. You good? What's wrong?" Charles inquired. He figured it had something to do with her situation with Sean from the way she answered the phone.

"Nothing I'm good thanks," Raquel quickly answered. She wasn't in the mood to talk about Keisha with Charles or anyone else.

She didn't want to be alone at the moment either, and going home was out of the question just in case Sean came back. Raquel was doing great when it came to her career, but her personal life was crumbling right underneath her feet. She decided to see what plans Charles had for the night, and hopefully they could just chill without any foolishness.

"Well, actually, are you busy tonight? I know we just got back but… I don't know," Raquel tried to explain. She didn't really know what she wanted from Charles at the moment but she didn't have anybody else to turn to. Her mother was out of the question; Brenda was not at all comforting in these types of situations, or any for that matter.

"Naw I'm chilling for the night, putting some trees in the air you know, the normal shit. I need to rap to you about something anyway. You coming over?" Charles asked.

It sounded like a plan to Raquel, but she decided no drinking this time. She didn't want another uncomfortable situation happening between them.

"Ok. Well whenever you ready for me to come over just hit my phone," Raquel said pulling into a gas station to fill up.

Charles was more than ready for Raquel to come over. He already had a plan set in motion, Raquel just beat him to the punch. Charles received some great news once he arrived back in Maryland and he wanted to share it with Raquel right away.

"You can come through whenever. The door will be unlocked. See you when you get here," Charles said hanging up the phone.

***

Keisha couldn't believe what just happened, she was in shock. This wasn't the first time she and Raquel had an argument, but this is the first time Raquel ever said anything about laying hands on her. If Dre would have just kept his mouth closed, none of this would have happened.

Keisha was fed up with Dre, and without thinking she charged out the room and went downstairs to confront him.

"What the fuck you open ya mouth for? And why the fuck was you standing outside the door? You petty ass nigga!" Keisha fumed. This was the last straw for her, Dre had to go. "I can't *believe* I married your stupid ass! Why me?"

Dre sat there in his recliner enraged. He thought he taught Keisha a lesson the last time he beat her ass, but obviously not. He got up, slowly walking over to Keisha. The expression on his face scared her and she immediately began to regret her tantrum. She did not want to be hit again, but at the same time she was tired of biting her tongue.

Dre was a fucking coward, he wouldn't dare hit another man but he wouldn't hesitate to hit her or any other woman. The more and more Keisha thought about all the things Dre put her through, the angrier she became.

As Dre approached Keisha, he didn't say a word. He let his hand do the talking. He punched her right in the mouth, causing her to fall to the ground. For good measure, he then proceeded to kick her a few good times.

Keisha was caught off guard. He would usually start off verbally before the abuse became physical. After the kicking stopped, Keisha hurried back onto her feet and ran for the stairs. She was going to get her keys and leave. Dre took off running right behind her, chasing her up the stairs, and when he got close enough, Dre grabbed one of her legs and pulled Keisha down the steps.

Keisha hit the stairs face first causing her nose to bleed instantly. She grabbed her gushing nose as her eyes filled with hot steamy tears from the pain. Keisha knew right now was not the time to feel pity for herself. She needed to get out the house before he possibly killed her.

Keisha rolled over onto her back and kicked Dre right in the nuts with both feet as hard as she could. Dre flew back down the stairs screaming out in agony as a tearful, bloody faced Keisha ran upstairs to get her belongings. She knew Raquel wasn't going to answer the phone so she decided she would just go straight to her house. Even if she wasn't there Keisha had a key and she knew no matter how angry her friend was with her, Raquel would not turn her away in her time of need.

Before she left the room, Keisha grabbed a bat out the closet just in case Dre was back on his feet ready to fight. When she ran out the bedroom, Dre was standing in the hallway holding his crotch. As soon as Keisha saw him she raised the bat in the air with a perfect home run stance. Dre was in too much pain to fight with her, he felt as if he had been kicked in the nuts by a horse!

"BITCH, JUST GET THE FUCK OUT!" Dre yelled at Keisha. She could hear the pain in his voice which made her crack a slight smile. She ran out the house with the bat still in her hand and hopped into her 2012 Honda Accord. She hit speeds up to eighty five miles per hour to make it to her best friend's house as fast as she could. Her nose was still bleeding and it hurt like hell. She was hoping the damn thing wasn't broken.

When she pulled up in Raquel's driveway she didn't see any lights on. *She must not be home,* Keisha thought. She went to the front door and entered the house using her key. It was beyond quiet inside the house.

"Raquel?" she called out timidly. Receiving no answer she went into Raquel's powder room to examine the damage to her face. She was starting to develop a black eye and her face was covered in dry and fresh blood. She grabbed some paper towels for her nose to avoid getting blood everywhere. She took a picture of her face with her phone just in case she needed the evidence.

I need to clean myself up. Keisha thought. She went upstairs and grabbed a towel and washcloth from the linen closet and ran the shower water in Raquel's guest bathroom. As Keisha removed her bloody clothes and placed them in the trash can, she became overwhelmed with emotion. She never pictured this type of life for herself. She always thought she would have a man who would love and cherish her, not a man who physically and verbally abused her every chance he got.

Keisha hopped into the hot steamy shower, feeling relieved as it began to relax her sore, achy body. The fall she had taken on the steps hurt her bad. Once the adrenaline wore off she could feel pain in almost every part of her body.

Keisha was starting to feel relaxed for the first time in days. The warm water was starting to melt layers of pain and anger away. She placed her head under the showerhead to wash her hair which also was slightly covered with blood. When she finished, she wrapped herself in a towel and walked down the hall to Raquel's room to look for something to throw on.

When Keisha opened Raquel's bedroom door, she was scared half to death! Sean was sitting on the bed looking like a madman.

"What the fuck you doing sitting in the dark? You didn't hear me hollering through this damn house?!" Keisha shrieked.

Sean was caught off guard himself. He was expecting to see Raquel walking through the door, not Keisha. He was also shocked to see her battered face.

"Yo, what the fuck happened to you? You alright?" Sean asked, sincerely concerned. With Raquel and Keisha being such close friends, he had also developed a friendship with Keisha over the years as well.

Keisha was embarrassed, she never let anyone see her like this before but she had no idea Sean was even there.

"Long story... And where is ya car? I didn't know you were even here. You scared the shit out me!" Keisha asked, trying to change the subject.

"I parked around the corner, I didn't want to Raquel to see my car. Ya crazy ass friend pulled a gun on me earlier. Here, meet me downstairs when you finished." Sean got up from the bed and grabbed Keisha something to put on and left out the room.

Once downstairs, Sean quickly called Raquel hoping she would answer but to no surprise she didn't. He tried a second time and again his call went unanswered. He knew Raquel wouldn't answer no matter how many times he called so he sent her a text message hoping she would at least read it.

Yo look I was here at the house waiting on ya crazy ass when Keisha walked in face all bloody. Get here now.

-Sean

Chapter 7

Charles went into the kitchen to check on the meal he was preparing for him and Raquel. He wasn't trying to rush her into a relationship, but he did want to show her he was definitely a better man than Sean.

The two men met a few times but didn't know each other very well at all. Charles only knew that Sean was a close friend of Raquel's, and he was a hustler. Charles had nothing against drug dealers. In fact, he had a very good relationship with one being as though he was a weed smoker, but he felt Raquel deserved more than a street nigga. He wanted to give her stability—a worry free life. She wouldn't have to look over her shoulder with him. All of his money was legit and he had lots of it. With Sean there was always the risk of death or jail because of his occupation and Charles didn't want that for Raquel.

Charles wanted to make sure everything was done before Raquel arrived. He didn't know she would be so willing to come over after he came on so strong in the limo, but whoever pissed her off was the person to thank.

He had less than an hour to finish up. The ride to Columbia wouldn't take her very long. Everything was pretty much set in place. The champagne was chilling in the ice bucket, dinner was finishing up in the oven, and the candles were already on the table, all he had to do was light them. He went upstairs to change into the clothes he laid out after his shower. He then sprayed himself with some cologne, brushed his waves, and checked his reflection in the mirror. If things went well tonight Charles would be on his way to the top as an agent. He may even have a new woman by his side.

Satisfied with his attire, Charles headed back downstairs to check on the food which he was sure should be done by now. Just as he hit the bottom stair, Raquel opened the unlocked door and walked into his welcoming home. She was amazed at what she saw. Charles had the whole place set up.

There was tall vase full of roses sitting the middle of the dinner table surrounded by unlit candles. She could smell something coming from the kitchen and whatever it was smelled delicious.

"Hey beautiful," Charles greeted as he walked up to Raquel and took her jacket, hanging it on the coat rack.

Raquel giggled. She should have known something was up. "So you mean to tell me you threw this together since we got off the phone?"

Charles laughed the question off. Instead of answering her, he walked her over to the table and pulled out a chair for her to sit. "I'll be right back," he said, disappearing into the kitchen.

He looked into the oven and removed the fully cooked meal, sitting it on the counter allowing it to cool. He also grabbed two champagne glasses and a lighter before going back to dining room. He sat the two glasses on the table and lit the candles that had a slight rosy scent them.

Raquel was impressed. Sean would never be capable of doing anything like this. He would rather buy gifts than put time, effort, and thought into something this romantic.

Charles filled the two glasses with champagne, handing one over to Raquel. "To a good night," he said, raising his glass for a toast. He couldn't wait to surprise her with the good news.

Raquel raised her glass and toasted to the night along with him.

"So do you want to talk about what had you so upset a lil' while ago?" Charles asked. He really wanted to be there for Raquel in any way he could, even if it was just a shoulder to cry on.

Up until this point Raquel hadn't thought twice about the whole ordeal with Keisha. Once she pulled off from Keisha's house she blocked it right out of her mind. The whole surprise dinner with Charles helped her forget about it as well.

"No not really. I don't want to focus my attention on stupid ass people right now," Raquel said, done with the situation for now.

"Ok. No problem. I'm just making sure you good. I'll be back, ma." Charles stood up from the table and walked back into the kitchen. He prepared two plates and returned to the table.

Raquel was pleasantly surprised when she saw Charles cooked one of her favorites. He made honey glazed salmon, sautéed shrimp, red roasted potatoes, and steamed broccoli. She had no idea he could cook like this. Their meal looked as if it was prepared by a professional chef. He made sure the plate was pleasing to look at, the presentation was wonderful.

"This looks amazing, thank you," Raquel said as Charles sat the plate in front of her. She couldn't wait to dig in. She hadn't eaten since she was on the plane coming back from LA.

"You're welcome. It's no big thing. I would cook for you every day if you let me," Charles said, kissing Raquel on the forehead before taking his seat. His soft lips sent a small tingle down her spine catching her off guard, but she played it off well.

This was not going to be another awkward night. At least she hoped not.

They sat at the table enjoying their meal when Raquel's phone began to ring but she decided to ignore it. She was not about to let anything or anyone ruin this moment. The food was delectable and their friendly conversation wasn't bad either.

"Damn!" Raquel yelled out in frustration as her phone beeped letting her know she had a new text message.

"See who it is baby. It might be an emergency," Charles suggested.

Raquel hesitantly took her phone out of her purse figuring it was Keisha, but to her surprise it was Sean. She didn't even bother reading the message.

"Who was it? Is everything ok?" he asked curiously.

Even though she didn't want to ruin the moment by bringing up Sean's name, Raquel wasn't one to tell lies, not even little ones. "It's nobody but Sean." She put the phone away and resumed her meal.

Charles wanted to know what was going on. He wanted to be with Raquel but if she was stuck on Sean he wasn't going to waste his time.

When her phone began to ring again, she pulled it back out expecting it to be Sean again. *I swear I'm about to lose it!* She thought angrily. This time it was in fact Keisha but she was in no mood to speak to her either so she sent the call straight to voicemail. A few seconds later a text message came in. She opened it up and what she saw devastated her.

Keisha sent Raquel the picture of her battered and bloody face.

"What's wrong everything ok?" Charles asked. He could see the panic and worry on her face as she read the text message.

Raquel was lost and confused. She was just with her friend and she was perfectly fine. She closed the message and opened Sean's text. She was hoping he hadn't taken his anger and frustration out on her friend. Raquel knew Sean very well and knew he wasn't capable of anything like this but after the last few stunts he'd pulled she wasn't going to put anything past him. Opening the message from Sean left her even more confused.

Yo look I was here at the house waiting on ya crazy ass when Keisha walked in face all bloody. Get here now.

-Sean

Raquel's eyes started to water as she began to grow more and more concerned for her friend. Even though she was angry at Keisha for keeping the baby situation a secret, she never wanted to see anything bad happen to her. She put her phone back in her purse and stood up from the table.

"I'm sorry. I gotta go. I'll call you later," Raquel told Charles as she began to cry.

Charles knew something major was going on. He just hoped she wasn't running off to be with Sean after he'd planned this special evening for them. If Raquel chose to be with Sean then that would prove she wasn't the woman he thought she was.

When they reached the front door, Charles helped Raquel put on her jacket. "Make sure you call me. I wanna make sure you ok." He said as he watched her walk out the door and off into the night.

***

Keisha wasn't surprised when Raquel sent her call straight to voicemail, but she was hoping she would at least look at the message she sent and call her back. She slipped on the clothes Sean gave her and headed downstairs.

Sean was sitting on the couch with a beer watching TV, so she went over to join him. Noticing Keisha, he turned the volume down on the television so they could talk. He was going to get to the bottom of this.

"Yo, so you gonna tell me or not? What happened to ya face?" Sean interrogated.

Keisha wanted to open up to someone and tell them all the things she had been going through over the years but she didn't want that person to be Sean. He had his own little part in the matter in Keisha's eyes. If he had just been straight up with Raquel then none of this would be going on.

"I just need to talk to Raquel," Keisha softly spoke.

Sean understood but he was also worried, he never saw Keisha like this before. He had a feeling she didn't get into it with a female because she could handle herself, even if it was more than one broad. He sat there looking at Keisha, her head was down and she looked sad and defeated.

"Was it Dre?" Sean asked, hoping he wasn't overstepping his boundaries.

Keisha was caught off guard by his question. She knew people weren't stupid but she didn't think that would be his first thought. Sean had the same look on his face everyone else did when they would see her. There was a time when Keisha was stopped by an old lady in the market who simply told her she deserved better. It was embarrassing to go out in public and be stamped as a victim of domestic abuse by total strangers.

Keisha couldn't hide it anymore. She was ready to speak up and since Raquel wasn't there she felt like she didn't have a choice to but let it out. She burst out in tears and shook her head 'yes' confirming Sean's allegations.

At that moment Sean felt like the scum of the earth. He regretted putting his hands on Keema after seeing Keisha in her condition. Sean gave her a hug to comfort her just as Raquel came storming through the front door.

"I was just trying to make her feel better," Sean said defensively as he jumped up from his friendly embrace with Keisha. He didn't want Raquel any madder than she already was.

Raquel was not at all bothered by their embrace. She was more concerned with what happened to her friend.

"Man, why the fuck are you back? And, Keish babe, what happened?" Raquel said, running over to her friend with tears of sadness running down her cheeks.

Keisha looked terrible. Her face was red and puffy. There was a small amount of blood running down her nose, her lip was busted, and she had a shiner under her right eye. Keisha just sat there and cried on her friend's shoulder. She held in so much pain and terror for so long that once she began crying she couldn't stop.

Raquel looked at Sean for clarity. At this moment he was the only person who may have known what was going on.

"She said it was Dre," Sean mouthed to Raquel.

Raquel sat back devastated. She grabbed her friend by the shoulders and looked her in the eyes before questioning her, "Keish, did Dre do this to you?"

Keisha continued to cry and again shook her head yes.

Raquel couldn't believe it. *How dare he put his hands on her!* "Was it because of the situation with this dumb ass nigga?" She cut her eyes at Sean.

"Yea," Keisha replied.

Sean continued to disappoint and hurt her. He had no idea how much all his bullshit with Keema was affecting everyone else around him.

Raquel sensed some tension when Dre came in the room while she and Keisha discussed the situation with Sean and Keema but she had no idea it would turn into this. She couldn't understand why Dre would get so upset. She assumed Keisha said something about his cousin to piss him off but that still wasn't an excuse. All sorts of things were running through Raquel's mind at the moment, she didn't know what to think.

Sean stood there confused. He had no idea how he had anything to do with this. He knew Dre and Keema were cousins but what the fuck did Dre beating Keisha's ass have to do with him? Raquel looked up at Sean and simply told him to leave which he did with no hesitation.

As Sean walked out the door, Raquel went into the kitchen to get Keisha a tall glass of ice water and some ibuprofen. She needed her friend to calm down and tell her what happened. She returned to the living room and handed Keisha two pills and the glass.

"Here take these. It will help with the pain." Raquel sat next to her best friend, rubbing her back comfortingly.

Keisha popped the pills in her mouth and chased them down with the water. She looked at Raquel, trying to muster up the strength to tell her about the secret life she had been living but she couldn't. It wouldn't be easy to confess yet another secret to Raquel. She knew how she felt about being left in the dark.

Raquel could see all the pain and hurt in Keisha's eyes. She wanted to help her friend but she wasn't exactly sure what happened. One thing was for certain: Dre was responsible and she didn't want her friend to go back to him, but right now wasn't the time to focus on that.

"Bestie, tell me what happened. What's going on?" Raquel asked sincerely.

Keisha took a deep breath and prepared herself to come clean.

"Dre has been beating on me pretty much since we met. I been hiding it all this time from you and everyone else because I was scared and embarrassed. Last year I was pregnant and he kicked me in my stomach. I-I-I miscarried but I married him because I thought he changed. I have to get away from him, Ra. Please help me!" she pleaded.

Raquel sat there complete in shock. She had no idea any of this was going on. She felt bad for her friend but she was also starting to feel like she didn't know the person sitting in front of her. Raquel and Keisha had been best friends since they were kids. Raquel always confided in Keisha, she told her everything and vice versa, or so she thought.

Raquel didn't want to make this about her but she couldn't help being a little upset. This made her feel like their friendship wasn't as tight as she thought. It was as if Keisha didn't trust her enough to tell her about this until things got this bad. This was a secret she had been keeping for the last three years.

Raquel just couldn't understand it. She needed something to calm her nerves, she didn't want to go off on her friend and make her feel any worse than she already did. "I'll be right back yo." Raquel stood up from the sofa and walked upstairs.

Heading into her bedroom, Raquel grabbed everything she needed to roll up. After she finished, she sat on the edge of the bed and reflected on the last few days. She could understand why Keisha would want to hide it from everyone else but she couldn't understand why her best friend didn't come to her for help a long time ago.

Maybe this is why she always kept Dre away from everyone, she thought. Maybe this was why she always had a strange feeling about him.

Raquel went into the bathroom to splash some cold water on her face before rejoining Keisha downstairs. She handed the blunt to Keisha and plopped down on the sofa.

Keisha lit it, lying back on the sofa trying to relax when she felt a sharp pain in her side. "Ahh! Shit that hurt!" she yelled out holding her side.

Raquel just shook her head feeling sorry for her. She didn't want to see her in pain like this. "Tell me what happened Keisha," she urged.

Keisha passed the blunt and took a drink of water before speaking. "After you left the house me and Dre got into it because I was mad he told you I knew about Keema being pregnant. I did know at Mo's but I wasn't sure. I wanted to see if it was true but when I got home that night Dre beat me. He was mad I spent our first night back home with you instead of with him so I never got the chance to ask about it." Keisha tried to explain as best as she could without going into detail.

Raquel just sat there looking at Keisha in disbelief. This was too much for her to handle all at once. "Regardless if you knew for sure or not you shoulda told me." She threw her hands up in the air frustrated. "And then all this shit about Dre? I thought we was cool. You supposed to be my bitch and come to find out you keeping secrets? I've told you so much personal shit about me and my life and I don't know shit that's going wit you. If I knew it was like this I wouldn't have told you shit," Raquel shouted.

Raquel was angry because she'd shared all her deepest dark secrets with Keisha, nothing was off limits. As kids Keisha would tell Raquel everything, even things her mom would make her do in order to get drugs. There was a point in time where they shared everything. Raquel was unaware that somewhere down the line that changed.

Keisha knew Raquel would be upset. They had vowed to always tell each other everything but Keisha hadn't been totally honest with her friend, and she didn't have a reason why. Raquel never shared any of her secrets or used them against her like other people in her life.

"I'm sorry I didn't tell you, Raquel. It was just easier to hide it. It's not that I don't trust you but... I don't know man." Keisha said sounding defeated.

Raquel was over it, she didn't want to talk about it anymore, and she didn't want to find out any more secrets. She was starting to feel like Keisha wasn't trustworthy. If she was keeping two huge secrets from her then there was no telling what else Keisha could be hiding.

"Do you need to go to the hospital?" Raquel asked dryly. She was pissed with Keisha but she wanted her to be ok.

"No. I'm fine. I just need to get away from him. This has been going on way too long." Keisha shook her head, disappointed with herself. Keisha was hoping even though Raquel was upset with her, she would still help her because she had no one else to turn to. Her mother died of a drug overdose years ago and she never knew her father.

"Well if you told somebody you were in trouble you could've had help a long time ago but you hid it instead. How the fuck did I not know?!" Raquel spoke out loud, talking to herself rather than Keisha.

Raquel was starting to question herself as a friend. *Was it something I missed? Did I not pay enough attention to Keisha to recognize a change in her?* Maybe this was what Keisha's text for help was about. Raquel regretted not calling Keisha back when she received her text in LA.

"When I had bruises and stuff I would cover it up with makeup and clothes or I would say I'm going on vacation. You couldn't have known, Ra," Keisha explained, not wanting her friend to blame herself.

Keisha regretted not telling Raquel sooner because she wouldn't be in this mess right now just like she said.

The more Raquel heard, the angrier she became. "Wow! Really? Vacation, huh? Then you was pregnant last year and didn't tell me? That's crazy, yo. You know all my secrets. You the only person that knew about my abortion, you took me! And you were pregnant and didn't mention it? How far were you?" Raquel questioned, fuming with anger.

Keisha didn't want to answer the question but she didn't want to keep lying to her one and only true friend either. She paused for a moment looking at Raquel, hoping she wouldn't lose her friend behind all this.

Raquel had been through a lot in her childhood with Brenda. Her mother consistently lied to her and disappointed her which left Raquel with serious trust issues. Keisha was fully aware of all these things which is why she wasn't sure if she should tell her the whole truth or not.

"I was about two and a half months. I found out when you were recovering after the abortion. I went back to see the doctor after you went in for the procedure," Keisha softly confessed.

Raquel just shook her head not knowing what to say. She didn't care for the conversation anymore so she acted as if Keisha hadn't said a thing and relit the blunt.

Raquel's success was being overshadowed by all this drama in her life. She hadn't even been able to share all her good news with the two people she cared for most because they were busy stabbing her in the back.

Raquel stuck her arm out to pass Keisha the blunt but as Keisha leaned over to take it, she yelled out in pain. Once again she grabbed her side, causing the blunt to hit the floor. Raquel quickly picked it up to avoid the carpet form being burned. She could tell there was something wrong that ibuprofen couldn't fix, so she decided she was going take Keisha to the ER regardless of what she said.

"Get up. We going to the hospital," Raquel demanded.

Even though Keisha did not want to go she knew it was in her best interest, she was in excruciating pain! Her side was killing her and her swollen nose didn't feel the greatest either. So the ladies gathered their things and slowly headed out the front door.

Chapter 8

Charles sat at the dinner table by himself looking at the two plates still sitting there and the empty chair across from him. He was starting to rethink his decision to pursue a relationship with Raquel. He was starting to realize she wasn't interested in being with him. She wanted to continue to chase Sean which was fine. Charles wasn't upset with her but he was very disappointed.

It had been a little over an hour since Raquel left and he hadn't heard anything from her. Charles cleaned off the table, disposed of all the food, candles, roses, and champagne and decided to call it a night. He went upstairs to his bedroom to look over some paperwork and emails. He also needed to fax the contracts they'd received in LA to the lawyers. Before he got started, he pulled out his phone to send Raquel a quick text.

Just making sure you good, hit me as soon as you get a chance we got business to discuss.

-Charles

At that moment Charles had decided to go with his gut instinct and keep it strictly professional between the two of them. It wouldn't be easy but it was the right decision for him on a personal and professional level.

***

Sean was confused as he left Raquel's house. He couldn't understand how he had anything to do with Keisha and Dre getting into it. He pushed the thought out of his mind and picked up the phone to call Reuben. Sean refused to keep living out of a hotel and DC wasn't his scene anyway.

Reuben agreed to meet him at the office within forty five minutes so Sean made his way in town. No matter what time, day or night, Rueben always came through.

The drive from Raquel's house to Reuben's office was only about twenty minutes, so once Sean arrived he sat in the empty parking lot and waited for the crooked realtor. Sitting there with nothing to do caused Sean's mind to drift back into thoughts of the beef with Keisha and Dre. He wished everything hadn't blown up in his face. He never thought it would get out of control like this. He couldn't even get Raquel to answer the phone for him these days. He texted her already knowing that more than likely he wouldn't get a response just like every other time.

I don't know what's going on wit ya girl but we need to talk, give me a chance to explain Ra.

-Sean

He continued to sit in the parking lot waiting for Reuben to arrive. As the minutes passed there was no response from Raquel. It wasn't a shock but it was eating Sean alive.

Reuben made it to the office in exactly forty five minutes just like he said and following him was the same black town car from before that would take them around to look at houses. Once both cars were parked, Sean got out of his Range and walked over towards them. Reuben got out of his Subaru and went over to the town car and opened the door for Sean to get in.

"Okay my man, let's see what we can find," Reuben said with a huge grin on his face. He was hoping Sean would like one of the properties he had lined up. If he did there would be a huge commission in store, not only for the sale of the house but for making everything look legal as well.

Sean got in car without saying a word. He had too much on his mind for small talk. All Sean wanted to do was conduct business and that was it. They drove downtown and entered into a small complex of condominiums not too far from the Inner Harbor. They looked nice from the outside but Sean wasn't impressed.

Canton was a quiet neighborhood in the city which was the perfect combination for him, but it wasn't the beautiful three-story home he once lived in. As they walked into the unit, Sean suddenly realized he was completely wrong. He had judged the property way too soon.

The place was beautiful, beyond anything he had ever seen. The condo was over forty three hundred square feet, spread out over four levels. It was a fully furnished waterfront property with an elevator, fireplace, a small in-home gym, three bedrooms, three full two half baths, and a two car garage. The master suite was secluded on the top floor with a huge balcony big enough to throw a party on facing the water. Everything about the space was lavish. All the appliances were up to date, the décor was different from level to level but the entire house flowed in perfect harmony.

After the tour Sean decided this was the place for him, he needed to look no further. The house was specular and there was more than enough room for him and the baby that may soon come. Everything about it was perfect, even the price was great. The only that was thing missing was Raquel.

"I'll take it, Reuben. How much money you need right now?" Sean asked pulling out two large bundles of money, one from each pocket.

Rueben didn't usually get excited by seeing large wads of money but it had been a while since he had seen so much cash on hand. As Rueben got older he lessened his criminal involvement which also limited his cash intake.

The listing price for the condo was 1.2 million dollars and Rueben needed at least half.

"I need six hundred thousand to get things rolling. We don't have to do this today. I will make sure the unit doesn't move for at least two weeks," Rueben offered.

Sean wasn't interested in holding off any longer. He needed a permanent place to stay and this was the one for him.

"Alright. Here you go. Where's the keys?" Sean said handing over the money. He had really come a long way. When he bought the decoy house it took him over a week to get the deposit together and now here he was standing here with every penny he needed.

Reuben handed over the keys and congratulated him on his new home. "I'll handle all the paperwork as usual, you just relax and enjoy." Reuben said shaking Sean's hand.

"Thanks for all ya help Ben. Now come on, let's go." Sean said not sounding as excited as Rueben expected.

Sean was glad he finally had a new place and things were moving forward but things weren't going as planned. The two men exited Sean's new condo and walked over to the town car that would take them back to Reuben's office. Sean didn't know what else to do about him and Raquel. Without her talking to him there wasn't much he could do. He had to figure this out and once he got back to his car, he would go pay Dre a visit.

***

Raquel and Keisha arrived at Northwest hospital within fifteen minutes of leaving the house. Raquel parked and walked her friend into the emergency room. They both walked up to the desk and were greeted by a heavyset middle aged woman.

"Hi, how can I help you?" the woman politely asked.

Keisha didn't answer the lady, she just looked over at her friend and by the look on Keisha's face, Raquel knew she needed to take over.

"My friend was attacked and she needs to be checked out." Raquel told the woman.

The lady looked at Raquel, then over at Keisha and proceeded to ask for her information.

The process seemed to take forever and the more time that passed, the more pain Keisha was starting to experience. As she answered the woman's questions her face ached with severe pain.

"Can you tell me where your pain is Miss Williams? Would you like to make a police report?" the lady questioned.

"No," Keisha quickly answered. She didn't want the police getting involved.

"It's mostly my nose and my side that hurts," Keisha told her.

"Is there a long wait?" Raquel asked, cutting off their conversation. She didn't want to spend all night in the hospital. She was exhausted.

The lady looked into the computer and informed them there were five people in front of Keisha but there was no way to estimate the wait time.

Raquel reached into her purse and pulled out five one hundred dollar bills and leaned over the counter. "Can you make this process go any faster? I would greatly appreciate it."

The receptionist looked around to make sure no one was looking at them and took the bills from Raquel's hand. The woman's eyes widened when she saw exactly how much she was given. "Umm, yes don't worry young lady. I'll put your friend here at the top of the list." She spoke in a whisper.

No sooner than they sat down in the waiting area, Keisha was being called into the back. There were a few moans and groans from the people who had been sitting there waiting before them, some for hours but Raquel wasn't concerned with any of that. All she wanted was to make sure Keisha was ok and go the fuck home.

The whole hour and a half they spent in the hospital Raquel didn't speak a word to Keisha. She used a small portion of that time to check her cell phone. She received two texts, one from Charles and one from Sean. She was in no mood for any more drama so she decided to read their texts in the morning.

Keisha's x-rays showed a small nose fracture which would heal on its own, and she also had some bruised ribs and bruised eye socket. The doctor prescribed her some pain medication and advised her to get some rest and to use lots of ice.

Raquel was livid with Keisha for allowing herself to be in this situation but she wasn't going to turn her back on her when her friend needed her most.

As the two women made their way to the car, Raquel finally decided to break her silence.

"So now that you added some more injuries to your list you ready to leave him or you good?" Raquel asked sarcastically.

Keisha knew her friend was mad but she thought she was being a bit harsh. She also knew that under Raquel's hard exterior deep down inside she meant well so Keisha didn't take it to heart.

"Yea I'm done for real this time," she said softly.

Raquel was hoping and praying Keisha would stand by her word but she wasn't so sure she would. After finding out Keisha took him back, *and* married him after he caused her to miscarry made Raquel have her doubts.

"You can move in with me. We'll go get ya stuff later when Dre isn't home," Raquel offered.

Keisha was relieved Raquel decided to put everything to the side and help her. She was truly grateful.

"Thank you, Ra. I know you not happy with me right but I promise I'll never keep anything from you again. I swear," she said with all sincerity.

"Uh huh." Was Raquel's only response.

***

As soon as they arrived back at Reuben's office Sean hopped back in his truck and took off towards The Village. He had been over to Keisha and Dre's house before so he knew exactly where to go.

Once Sean arrived he wasted no time getting out and knocking on the door. He needed to know what was going on. First Sean knocked lightly but there wasn't an answer, so he knocked a little harder and within a minute or two Sean could hear someone unlocking the door.

"Who the fuck is knocking on my... Oh wassup my nigga?" Dre said caught off guard as he swung the door open. Sean was the last person he was expecting to see. He knew this had to be about Raquel and Keisha arguing earlier.

"Can I come in? We need to talk," Sean asked cutting right to the chase.

"Yea come on in. How my cousin and ya unborn doing?" Dre said as he stepped aside letting him in.

Sean wasn't there to talk about any of that and Dre's casual attitude was already starting to piss him off. If Sean hadn't seen Keisha with his own eyes, he would have no idea about their fight from the way Dre was acting.

"Yo, I ain't come here to talk about that. What happened with you and Keisha?" Sean asked aggressively.

Dre wasn't expecting Sean to come in and question him about his wife. He figured this would be more about Raquel. He didn't count on Keisha going to anyone for help after their fight either. Keisha never told anyone, especially Raquel about their fights before and that's how he preferred it. Dre was actually waiting for Keisha to return back home like she always did. He really didn't know how to respond to Sean's question.

"I don't think that's any of ya business, homie. I don't get involved with whatever is going on with you and Keema. What Keisha got to do with you?" Dre asked, becoming defensive. He didn't know what to expect or what would happen next.

Sean didn't come for a confrontation but Dre was starting to push his buttons. He took a long deep breath before speaking. "Aye yo, chill wit' all that tough Tony shit. I'll bust ya ass in here. And I'm making it my business since my name was put in it, you bitch ass nigga! So what the fuck happened?!"

Sean was becoming impatient. He wanted to know why Raquel and Keisha felt like he had anything to do with what this clown ass nigga did.

Dre was a little hesitant to answer Sean's questions. He didn't want anything to pop off. Dre was a whore when it came to fighting a man. He already knew he wasn't any competition for Sean.

"I mean, Raquel came over and they started talking about you and Keema. Then they got into an argument and Keisha was mad at me cause Raquel left," Dre half-ass explained.

Sean's patience was getting thinner and thinner. He wasn't sure how much longer he could keep his composure. He knew it was more to it than that, it had to be.

"Look nigga, stop beating around the bush. I know you beat up Keisha and I'm tired of playing these games. What the fuck do that shit have to do with me?" Sean asked almost yelling.

"Look I don't know what the fuck it got to do with you but I'm a grown ass man, my dude. I don't have to answer to you. Fuck you!" Dre shouted in Sean's face. He wasn't about to let Sean treat him like a bitch in his house.

That was the last straw for Sean. He lost it.

He hopped over the coffee table and knocked Dre's ass right on the floor with one hit. Sean didn't stop there, he released all his pent up anger and frustration he had built up over the past few days. As Dre lay on the floor Sean kicked and stomped his face until it was covered with blood. He wanted him to look as bad as Keisha did, if not worse. "Think about this ass whooping before you put ya hands on another female, pussy!" he yelled, spitting on Dre as he exited the house.

Sean felt like the biggest hypocrite ever. The nerve of him to look down on Dre for beating on Keisha when he just recently put his hands on Keema. Even though Sean didn't harm Keema as much as Dre had Keisha, it was still wrong. Sean didn't want to get back with Keema in the slightest but he decided the right thing to do was apologize. It was time for him to handle things with her like an adult. He also needed to know what exactly was going on with the baby.

Sean hadn't talked to Keema since he dropped her off after the hospital visit. So he decided to jump in his whip and make his way over to Patterson Park in order to make things right with Keema for the sake of the child she would soon bear.

Within twenty minutes Sean was pulling up to the house, calling Keema's cell so she could unlock the door. She came downstairs, let him in, and turned right around to go back upstairs.

It was late and she wasn't in the mood to fight. All she wanted to do was get back in her bed and relax. The pregnancy, along with her nerves, was starting to take a toll on her.

Sean knew this wouldn't be the easiest thing for him but he had to do it. He shut and locked the front door and went upstairs to the bedroom he once shared with Keema. As he sat down on the edge of the bed Keema noticed his blood-stained Timberlands.

"What the hell happened to you?" Keema asked, looking down at his boots.

Sean hadn't even noticed the large amount of blood all over him. He couldn't tell her the truth about fucking up her cousin so he told a lie instead.

"Oh I got into it with some niggas, nothing major. So how you been feeling?" he asked trying to spark up a conversation, while going into the closet to change his shoes. Sean had plenty of stuff still there he needed to get and take to his new place.

Keema had no idea what Sean was up to but after the way he had been treating her she didn't want anything to do with him. She had even reconsidered her plan of getting back with him. It was clear Raquel was all he cared about and she was starting to accept that.

"Look Sean, it's nice of you to ask but don't act like you care about me or this baby," she snapped.

Sean wasn't even upset that she was giving him attitude. He had been a complete asshole the past few days. First he left her at the club to go home with Raquel and then he choked her even after she told him she was pregnant. As he sat there and thought it over, he felt like shit.

"Yo Keema, I'm sorry for the way I've been acting. Yea it's true I want to leave you for Raquel but it was wrong for me to take my anger out on you. I mean you could have handled things a lil' differently, too, but that doesn't excuse my behavior. I'm sorry." Sean said as he touched Keema's pregnant belly for the first time and something magical happened.

Keema felt the baby kick which was a first. She and Sean both looked up at each other as they felt the little life inside her move. Sean had never experienced anything like this before. He hadn't spent much time around pregnant woman in his life.

Keema was overcome with emotion. She never wanted to get emotionally connected to the fetus that she didn't plan on keeping but feeling movement inside her made her heart smile.

"Did you feel that? I've never felt the baby move before. He or she must know you they daddy," she said smiling from ear to ear.

Sean couldn't help but smile as well. He was starting to like the idea of being a father even though he knew he and Keema would never be together again.

"Come here," Sean said extending his arms out to hug Keema. She wasted no time jumping into his arms.

Feeling his embrace reminded her of why she loved him so much. Before all the drama Sean was the sweetest man she had ever met. He didn't judge her for her past and he even forgave her after a few infidelities. Right then and there she decided she would make things work and they would have a family. She was going to keep the baby and be the best woman and hopefully someday wife to Sean.

Keema rubbed her nose along the side of Sean's neck, taking in the scent of his cologne as they continued to embrace. She missed his presence and she wanted her man back. She climbed on top of Sean's lap and began to grind and kiss on him.

Sean jumped back, not wanting to get involved with Keema like that. All he wanted to do was have a civilized conversation with her so they could be co-parents.

"Aye yo what you doing? This ain't for us no more," he said turning her down, but Keema wasn't going to give up so easily. She knew exactly what to do in order to get Sean's attention.

"You don't want to give us one last try for the sake of the baby?" Keema asked while continuing to kiss Sean as she unzipped his pants.

Before he knew it Keema was on her knees giving him brain. She had a way of making men do whatever she wanted with her skills, which is how she got Sean in the first place. Keema continued to suck and lick all over Sean's dick as she gently massaged his balls. Sean gripped the sheets enjoying the sensation. He wasn't really focused on the person who was pleasing him but focused on the pleasure itself.

Keisha shoved his entire penis into her mouth and to the back of her throat. Once she did that Sean lost all control. He picked Keema up off her knees, threw her on the bed and began to not only fuck her but make love to her. The sex between them at that moment was the best it had been in months. All thoughts of Raquel left Sean's mind for a moment as he was in heaven right between Keema's thighs.

Keema was enjoying herself too. It had been a while since Sean touched her like this. The way he stroked her made her entire body shiver. She was hoping this would be the start of a new beginning for them and their new family.

Sean figured since Keema was already pregnant there was no need to pull out, so he released his cum inside of her and collapsed. This would be the last time he would ever sleep with Keema. He made it clear who he wanted to be with and Keema wasn't it. As long as this doesn't get out to Raquel everything would be fine. Even If Keema told Raquel they had sex, it would be her word against his. Sean would just tell her Keema was making it up in order to break them apart for good.

Sean rolled over to the other side of the bed and went to sleep as if Keema wasn't even there. Keema noticed how distant he was being but she wasn't worried. She figured he would come back around eventually. She planned on getting up early in the morning to cook Sean's favorite; French toast covered in powdered sugar and scrambled eggs with cheese. For now she would just lie next to Sean and dream about their future.

Chapter 9

When Keema awoke the next morning, she noticed Sean was no longer there. She got up to see if he was in the bathroom or downstairs but he was nowhere to be found. She looked out the window and saw that Sean's truck was also gone so she picked up her phone and called him.

"Hey baby, where did you go? I was going to make you some French toast," Keema said charmingly.

Sean was starting to regret the breakup sex with Keema. It did exactly what he didn't want it to and that was give Keema hope for a future with him.

"Look yo, last night was fun and all but I told you who I wanna be with. I'll be a good father but that's as far as it goes. You can have the house. I got a new spot for myself and there is plenty of room for the kid so we good." He said slowly crushing every piece of Keema's heart. She couldn't believe what she was hearing. She thought last night would change his mind, even if just a little but it hadn't.

"You got ya own spot? So why didn't you take ya raggedy ass home instead of sleeping here with me? You know what— fuck you Sean. I don't need you. Fuck you!" Keema said hanging up the phone.

She was beyond pissed, she was *hurt*. At that moment she lost all hope for her and Sean. There was no way she was going to keep running behind a man who didn't want her.

Keema sat there not knowing how to handle her emotions. She felt everything from anger to sadness, to loneliness and hate. She decided since Sean wanted to play with her life and feelings, she would return the favor.

***

The next morning Raquel woke up and felt as if she had been drinking the previous night. Her head was pounding and she had the worse headache ever. Forcing herself out of the bed, she went down the hall to check on Keisha.

Raquel quietly opened the door and found her friend still sleeping, so she decided to let her rest. She went downstairs and began to prepare a quick breakfast for her and Keish. She whipped up some fluffy buttermilk pancakes, maple flavored bacon, and eggs scrambled with onions and cheese. She placed Keisha's plate in the microwave and began to eat.

By the time Raquel wrapped up her meal Keisha was just walking into the kitchen following the smell that had awakened her.

"Morning boo, what smells so good?" Keisha said halfway smiling, still in pain.

Raquel was still in her feelings so she didn't have much to say.

"Ya plate is in the microwave," she offered, getting up and walking back upstairs. Raquel went into her room and grabbed her cell phone so she could return Charles's text from last night.

Raquel never did let him know she was okay. With everything that happened, it totally slipped her mind. She was hoping Charles wasn't upset with her for leaving early last night. He was really starting to win her over and she wanted to entertain the thought of them dating as soon as things in her life calmed down.

Raquel dialed Charles's number and it rang until the voicemail picked up. It was rather early so she thought maybe he was still sleep. After the beep she left Charles a brief message, "Hey Charles, sorry about last night. I had to go help a friend. I'm free to talk whenever you are. Call me."

Raquel really wanted to know about the business he wanted to discuss but she would just have to wait until Charles returned her call. Then there was a text from Sean. She was still totally confused about what to do.

She couldn't really be mad that Keema was pregnant, that did happen before she came along but she didn't like being played. Sean ducked and dodged her calls and on top of that she heard about the baby from Keema, not him. To Raquel that was the ultimate betrayal. She decided to think on it before she answered any of Sean's many attempts to contact her. Maybe they needed to talk and clear the air but Raquel wasn't so sure that was the right answer. Then there was the situation with Keisha and Dre. She also needed to clear the air with her friend, especially since she was going to living with her now.

Raquel took a deep breath and went back downstairs to the kitchen to speak with Keisha. They needed to get their friendship back on track and plan Keisha's escape from Dre. Raquel entered into the kitchen and found Keisha staring at the plate of food sitting in front of her. Raquel never saw Keisha look so sad and helpless in her life, and she sincerely felt bad for her friend.

"Hey Keish, what's wrong? You not hungry?" Raquel asked trying to break the tension between them.

"I'm just feeling a lil' down. I can't believe I let things go on like this and I know you mad but you have to believe me. I didn't tell you about Dre because I was embarrassed. It never got this bad before. The miscarriage was the real first big thing," Keisha said trying to justify her secrecy.

Raquel was starting to see things from Keisha's perspective just a little but she still couldn't understand why she was too embarrassed to come to her. Raquel thought it sounded more like an excuse than an explanation.

"I hear you but there isn't anything I wouldn't come to you with. I trusted you with everything but I guess we just different. Look, don't trip, we good. I just want you to stay away from him this time. When do you think we can get ya stuff?"

Keisha knew Raquel wasn't hundred percent over everything but she was glad her friend was willing to move forward. She got up to hug Raquel. She was really grateful for her. Hugging Raquel also reminded her she needed to take some pain medication, her body was still very sore.

"Oh, I'm sorry. Did I hug you too tight? Let me get ya meds," Raquel said, noticing how Keisha tensed up during their embrace.

Keisha giggled, loving how attentive her friend was. It felt good to have someone who cared for her well-being. Dre never took care of Keisha when she was sick or in pain.

"Naw. I'm good for now. I need to eat this breakfast you cooked first but we can go to the house tonight. Dre isn't usually home." She was ready to leave Dre and that house of bad memories behind forever.

"Ok cool. We gonna hit his stash too so I can have me a nice weed supply. We gonna teach his ass a lesson," Raquel said laughing although she was very serious. She loved the drug and if she could take Dre off it would make her feel even better. They would be getting some type of payback for all the things he put Keisha through.

"Sounds good to me, fuck that bitch!" Keisha said slapping high fives with Raquel.

Keisha began to eat her food and Raquel went upstairs to dress for the day.

"When you finished get dressed!" Raquel yelled walking up the stairs. She planned on surprising Keisha with a nice girl's day out. They were going to enjoy manicure, pedicures, full body massages, and whatever else they felt like doing. Raquel knew Keisha could use the relaxation and after all the drama that had been going on, so could she. Raquel was beat down and she could definably use a pick me up. After pulling out a comfortable pair of sweat pants and a t-shirt Raquel hopped in the shower.

After about a good thirty five minutes of cleansing her body and standing under the hot shower water, Raquel finally stepped out throwing her hair in a ponytail and throwing on her clothes. She opened the bedroom door and stuck her head into the hallway, "Keisha, you done eating yet? Get dressed nigga, you about to miss the cypher!"

Keisha could hear her loud and clear, she was already done with breakfast, freshly showered, and dressed by the time Raquel finished with her unusually long shower. She was always finished before Raquel no matter how much of a head start she got.

"You better not start without me I'm coming now!" Keisha yelled back. She was carefully putting on her makeup in order to cover the bruising caused by the incident with Dre. This would be the last time Keisha looked at herself in the mirror and saw a battered woman. She wanted to wear makeup only when she wanted to, not because she had to. She set her foundation with translucent powder and headed down the hall to Raquel's room.

As she opened the bedroom door she found Raquel sitting on the bed pearling. Keisha wasted no time jumping up on the bed next to her friend not wanting to miss out. Raquel sparked the weed filled cigar for them to enjoy before leaving out for the day.

The two friends sat back enjoying the cypher, talking and reminiscing as if nothing happened between them. As they continued to laugh and joke, Raquel's phone began to ring. She looked at the screen to see who was calling and when she saw

Sean's name appear on the screen. She sucked her teeth and passed Keisha the blunt.

"Who was that?" Keisha asked as she inhaled the smoke.

"Girl, Sean. I haven't been answering any of his calls or texts since I found out everything in LA," Raquel informed Keisha.

Keisha didn't want to speak on the subject, not wanting to stir up any ill feelings but she couldn't resist. "Ra, why don't you talk to him, at least once? You owe y'all friendship that if nothing else."

Raquel didn't respond. She just sat there quietly thinking and Keisha did have a point. Her and Sean had been through a lot. It seemed wrong to let it go down like this but she just wasn't ready.

"I don't know... Maybe later, let's go." Raquel said dismissively snatching the blunt from Keisha, running down to the garage.

The two friends were on their way to start a day of full of relaxation and the first stop would be the nail salon.

***

Charles was suddenly awakened by the sound of his cell phone buzzing on the nightstand. He rolled over and grabbed the phone seeing that he had a few missed calls and a voicemail from Raquel. He wasn't in the mood to deal with her right now. Charles was still a little salty about last night. He didn't expect to feel any type of way about Raquel leaving the dinner but he did despite telling himself he would handle business with her and that's all.

Charles listened to the voicemail and hearing Raquel's voice hit a soft spot with him. It was just something about her that was simply irresistible but he brushed the feeling off immediately.

He dialed Raquel's number in order to call and make arrangements for a quick meeting. The phone rang until Raquel finally answered the phone.

"Hey boo wassup?" Raquel said, happy that Charles returned her call so quickly. She wanted to talk to him about last night and make it up to him. Instead of Charles cooking and making the night special for her, she wanted to do that for him.

"Ain't nothing. I just got ya message so I wanted to see when you were free," Charles said nonchalantly.

Raquel could sense there was something wrong. Even though they didn't know each other too well on a personal level, they spent so much time together conducting business so she knew his personality very well. She figured he was a little upset about last night but it was something out of her hands.

"My friend and I are on our way out. I'm sorry I had to leave last night. I'll make it up to you though," she said seductively.

Even though he wanted to, Charles wasn't even going to entertain the idea. It went in one ear and out the other.

"Well just hit me when y'all done so we can meet up and talk. I'll holla at you later," he said before hanging up the phone, completely ignoring Raquel's advance.

***

Raquel looked at the blank screen in disbelief. She was surprised Charles hung up on her and didn't even mention anything about her offer. She sucked her teeth and rolled her eyes putting the phone down. Today was the day she was going to relax with her childhood friend and leave all the drama behind.

"Who was that? Did I interrupt something last night?" Keisha asked, being nosey. She hoped she hadn't disturbed her night too much.

"Oh that was my agent Charles," Raquel said, quickly dropping the topic. She was hoping after they talked about what happened last night Charles would understand and lose the attitude.

Raquel turned off Liberty Road and into a shopping center where they would get their nails done. Raquel parked and the two friends walked into the nail shop. There were already a few people getting serviced but it wasn't busy at all. Raquel requested two pedicures and two manicures for them.

"Would you like eyebrow?" the short Chinese lady asked.

"No, thank you. We're ok," Raquel politely declined.

The little lady escorted them to the back of the nail shop where the pedicure chairs were. The ladies took off their shoes, rolled up their pants legs and sat comfortably in the massage chairs as the woman filled the bowls up with warm water.

After a few short minutes, two younger women came over to start Raquel's and Keisha's pedicures. The two friends sat back and relaxed as they began rehashing the Keisha and Dre situation. Keisha told Raquel the entire story with every detail. It actually felt good for her to get everything off her chest. She was tired of holding everything in and dealing with all these emotions alone. Getting it out was giving Keisha some much needed closure. Raquel sat there listening to every single word not passing any judgment. She was over being angry. All she wanted to do now was be a good friend and supporter.

After their pampering was finished, Raquel paid the tab and they headed out. Their next destination would be the Red Door Spa in Cross Keys.

***

Charles was beginning to get impatient. He knew Raquel was out enjoying herself but in his mind business trumped everything. He needed her to be packed and on a plane to the Bahamas tomorrow! Jacquelyn had also called and wanted to set up an hour long meeting with the two of them. He needed Raquel to get more involved with her career before it disappeared right before her eyes. Models came a dime a dozen and she needed to keep working while she was in high demand.

Charles needed to speak to her tonight and if she had plans they would just have to wait. He picked up the phone and dialed Raquel's number. The phone rang and rang until he was greeted by the voicemail.

"Hey Raquel, we got money to make. I need you packed and ready to get on a plane. Plus Jacquelyn called so holla at me." He also sent Raquel a text message letting her know the voicemail he left was urgent.

This time around he would do things differently and sit most of this trip out. Raquel was a big girl and he didn't need to chaperone her. He sat at his dining room table impatiently waiting for Raquel to return his call. In the meantime he was going to think of other candidates to present for the project just in case Raquel didn't come through in time.

***

Raquel and Keisha spent the twenty five minute drive continuing to chit chat, enjoying each other's company. As they arrived and walked inside the spa Keisha was in awe. She had never been there before and the place was absolutely beautiful. She really loved all the red accents around the place. Raquel also loved it there too. It was one of her favorite spots to visit. The milk and honey body treatment was her favorite but today she was just keep it simple and get a massage.

Once the woman selected their services the staff wasted no time getting to business. Raquel chose to have the Swedish massage and Keisha would indulge in a deep tissue massage. She made sure to warn the therapist not to massage her bruised ribs since they were still very sore.

Both women were deeply relaxed as they enjoyed their massages and the aromatherapy candles burning around them. The hour and twenty minute session felt like it could last forever. Everything was quiet and peaceful and that's exactly what these women needed.

"That was the best, bitch thank you! I coulda paid for it though." Keisha offered. She was grateful but she felt like Raquel had done enough by rescuing her and taking her into her home.

"Oh it's nothing, I wanted to treat you. You can save ya coins and move ya ass out of my house," Raquel said, joking with her friend.

Keisha burst out laughing loud as usual and playfully pushed her friend. "Fuck you bitch."

"How about some lunch?" Raquel suggested. She was starving. They hadn't eaten since breakfast earlier that morning.

"Bet. Where we going? I'm hungry as hell. Kona Grill?" Keisha suggested.

"Sounds good to me, let's go."

The two women got into the truck and took off towards the Inner Harbor. Raquel pulled into a parking garage on Pratt Street and walked over to the restaurant.

Raquel and Keisha found two empty seats at the bar where they sat and ordered drinks while reviewing the menu.

"Today was a good day! I needed that! I'm glad we got past all of this too." Keisha said realizing how good of a friend Raquel really was.

"It took me a few but I'm good. I just have to realize everyone ain't me." Raquel said throwing some shade, but she couldn't help it. It was just her nature to be sarcastic.

Keisha just giggled, picking up on the jab. As they tried to decide on what to order, Raquel's phone began to ring. Her phone hadn't rung all day but she knew it would happen eventually. She looked at the screen and right away all her stress came back.

"Girl, it's Sean calling me AGAIN." Raquel told said while rolling her eyes.

"Just answer the damn phone and talk to the man," Keisha yelled out.

Raquel laughed at her friend's loudness. She swore Keisha only did that when they were out in public.

She let the phone continue ringing but promised to call Sean after they placed their orders.

The young waiter came over with their drinks and waited for the ladies decisions.

"I want the grilled salmon salad, please." Raquel requested.

"And I would like to have an order of potstickers." Keisha said while still looking into the menu. She didn't want to make eye contact with anyone knowing her injuries were still noticeable despite the makeup.

"Ok. I'll be back with your food as soon as it's ready." He informed them before taking off.

Raquel pulled out her phone and took a deep breath before returning Sean's call. She needed to prepare herself for this.

"Hello?" Sean said sounding surprised. He thought Raquel would never answer the damn phone or return his many attempts to contact her.

Raquel couldn't even front, hearing Sean's deep raspy voice made her feel some type of way, but she wasn't going to act as if none of this drama didn't happened.

"Yea, yo, wassup?" Raquel asked nonchalantly.

"Ra, please let me come over and talk to you. I need the chance to explain... How's Keisha?" Sean asked.

Raquel wasn't ready. Even though she had given it a lot of thought, she was feeling pressured by him and Keisha to talk. Everybody was worried about his feelings and not hers.

"She's right here. You can ask her yaself," Raquel said passing Keisha the phone, escaping the conversation.

Keisha shot Raquel the look of death as she snatched the phone away from her. Raquel was supposed to be calling Sean to talk to him, not her.

"Hey Sean, wassup?" Keisha asked.

"Nothing much, I was just checking on you. How you feeling? I went to go see ya mans." He told her, and Keisha knew what that actually meant.

"What? When?" Keisha asked wanting to know the details. She was shocked Dre hadn't called her talking shit. Sean must have really fucked him up.

"Look yo, I'mma be at the house when y'all get there. Don't tell ya crazy ass homegirl. You got me?" Sean was going to make Raquel talk to him whether she wanted to or not.

"Yea I'm ok but I'mma talk to you later, we about to eat." Keisha said trying to speak in code. She hung up the phone and stuck it in Raquel's purse.

"Well what he say?" Raquel wanted to know if he said anything about her.

"I don't know. Maybe you shoulda stayed on the phone." Keisha said rolled her eyes.

Raquel burst out in laughter. She almost forgot how much of a smartass Keisha could be. The girls spent the reminder of the afternoon eating, laughing and drinking. After they finished up, Keisha paid the tab and left the waiter a generous tip. She thought that was the least she could do after all the money Raquel spent throughout the day.

Before pulling out the garage, Raquel grabbed her cell phone so she could play some music. Looking at her phone, she saw a text and voicemail message from Charles. She listened to the message and was excited yet confused at the same time.

Raquel wasted no time picking up the phone and returning his call to find out more. He must have been waiting for her because he picked up on the second ring.

"Wassup yo, where you been all day?!" Charles asked sounding irritated. He hated waiting on models to return his phone calls when it came to gigs and Raquel was no exception. Sometimes if you waited too long the offer could be pulled right from under you. Nothing was final until there was a signed contract.

"Damn, my bad. I told you I was wit my homegirl." She tried to explain but Charles didn't care. Time was money and Raquel was wasting both.

"I hear you yo, but this is more important. You could have texted a nigga back to set up a time to meet or something!" Charles lectured.

Raquel hadn't even noticed that he called or texted until now but she wasn't going to keep explaining herself. All she wanted was to know what was so damn important. "Alright yo. I'll drop my friend off and then meet you at ya house."

"Naw I'll meet you at the Starbucks by ya house. I gotta come out there anyway." Charles lied. He just didn't want Raquel to come over because he wasn't sure if he could resist her. He would rather just get the contracts signed and go back home.

Raquel didn't know what his issue was. She wasn't sure if it was the personal or the business things that were the real issue, or maybe it was a little bit of both. This surprisingly didn't discourage Raquel from wanting to purse a relationship with Charles. She knew no relationship was perfect and as long as he wasn't shutting her out or keeping money out her pocket she was cool. All the other little things they could work on.

Raquel decided she was going to be more focused on business from here on out. She loved her friends and all but she had herself to worry about. "Ok. I'll call you when I'm on my way to Starbucks." Raquel said before hanging up the phone.

Keisha sat back, not helping but to overhear her conversation. "You going out tonight?"

Damn. We were supposed to get her things from the house while Dre's gone. Raquel remembered. She figured that was the source of Keisha's question. "Oh, I'm sorry boo. Can we go by the house some time tomorrow? I gotta go meet my agent."

Raquel felt bad, she totally but it wasn't like Keisha reminded her either.

Keisha had actually forgotten about getting her things, the day had been so perfect that she hadn't thought about anything else. She really did not want to go back into that house, but she had to get her clothes if nothing else.

"Ok that's cool, no big thing. I need to go take some meds and lay down anyway." Keisha said reclining back in the passenger seat.

They hopped on the JFX and headed back to Owings Mills. Raquel would drop Keisha off and go meet Charles... or so she thought...

Chapter 10

Sean arrived at Raquel's home and made himself comfortable. On the way there he stopped at a flower shop and picked up some gifts for both women. He had a small brown bear holding a tiny balloon that read "Feel Better" for Keisha. And a big white teddy bear holding a big red heart that read "I'm Sorry" and a vase full of roses for Raquel.

He was hoping this would break the ice and make Raquel more willing to talk to him. He also stopped and picked up some food for them from Boston Market and wine from the liquor store. Sean was trying to pull out all the tricks he could. He was very nervous. Raquel had become unpredictable these days. He still couldn't believe she pulled a gun out on him.

Sean was there for about thirty five minutes before hearing the garage slowly creep open. He stood in the kitchen waiting for Raquel and Keisha to walk into the house. As they got out of the car Sean could hear them closing the doors and Raquel talking.

"Imma run in here and use the bathroom then I gotta dip. Let me text him now," he overheard Raquel saying to Keisha.

As they entered the house Sean bum rushed Raquel with a ton of questions. "Where you going and who is he?" he asked feeling extremely jealous. He knew she couldn't have moved on that fast. To his knowledge, there wasn't anyone in her life before him.

Raquel stopped dead in her tracks. She was tired of Sean popping up unannounced. She knew there was no way he was going to give up his keys so she would have to change the locks.

"What the fuck are you doing here? I shoulda shot you right in the ass!" Raquel said as she walked into her powder room.

Sean's plans never seemed to work out. He felt like the universe was against him. Maybe this was karma. He figured by the time he would finally get a chance to talk to Raquel it would be too late.

"Where she going yo?" Sean asked trying to pry information out of Keisha but she did not want to get in involved. She did her part now the rest was up to him.

Keisha just shrugged her shoulders and began to walk upstairs minding her business.

"Hold up I got something for you and ya friend," he said walking into the living room where he had the gifts.

Sean handed Keisha the little bear and she was touched. It meant a lot to her that everyone was being so comforting and supportive during all of this. "Thank you, Sean. This is sweet.

Maybe you should stick around for a lil' while. I'm sure Ra will love her gifts when she gets back." Keisha said admiring the beautiful teddy bear and crystal vase full of bright red roses in the corner.

She always wished Dre did things like that for her, which is why she wanted Raquel to at least hear Sean out. Good men were rare and she thought they just happened to try things with each other at the wrong time.

"Thanks Keish. I'm glad somebody is pushing for me." Sean said feeling a little down. Keisha gave Sean a hug and headed upstairs.

Raquel came out of the bathroom, rushing towards the garage. Sean darted into the kitchen, just barely catching Raquel before she slipped out the door.

"Hold on Ra. Just give me five minutes," he pleaded.

Raquel really didn't have time for this. She had to go meet Charles and she didn't want to piss him off any more than he already was. She texted him saying she would be there in ten which was about five minutes ago.

"You got two minutes so hurry up. What is it you so desperately need to say?" Raquel said with an attitude.

"Look Ra, I just want to explain. I wasn't trying to keep the baby a secret or hide it but I knew you wasn't having it. I was just trying to think of how to tell you. Yeah I fucked up, I know I did but it's not what you think. That morning I left here and went home was the first I heard about the baby. I packed my shit and left. I was staying in a hotel in DC but I just got a new place last night." Sean poured his heart out trying to get Raquel to see things from his point of view.

Raquel didn't know what to think. She wanted to believe him but she just wasn't sure.

Sean saw the look of uncertainty on her face and walked over to Raquel, kissing her gently. She could feel herself falling for him all over again. Sean scooped Raquel off her feet and carried her into the living room. They began to make love, causing Raquel to forget all about her meeting with Charles.

***

Charles received Raquel's message saying she would be at the Starbucks in ten minutes but he was more than twenty five minutes away. He figured with all the time Raquel wasted, he could make her wait for a few minutes. He made sure everything he needed was in his briefcase before slipping on his shoes and heading out the door.

He hopped on the highway and made his way to Raquel's side of town, praying she agreed to do the Bahamas project. This would be a big deal for both of them. Charles had never done any work outside the U.S so this would get him recognized on a whole different level as an agent. He wouldn't stay the entire trip but he would be there the day of the shoot to show his face and network with potential clients.

He parked in the lot in front of Starbucks and walked inside to look for Raquel. As he entered the coffee shop, to his surprise Raquel was nowhere in sight. He was beginning to get fed up with her. She wasn't being dedicated and focused like she usually was.

Charles sat down at one of the empty tables and pulled out his phone to call Raquel. The phone rang and rang until the voicemail answered his call. He tried a second time and again, the same thing happened. He was furious!

Raquel texted him over a half hour ago saying she would meet him there in ten minutes and wasn't there! Charles wasn't having it. If Raquel continued this behavior, she would have to find herself a new agent. He gathered his things and decided to pay her a home visit.

***

As Sean and Raquel continued to make love on the couch, she noticed a pair of headlights creep up her driveway. She almost jumped out of her skin when she realized it was Charles. She didn't know what had become of her. She never put any man before her paper. She zipped up her pants and tried to fix herself as much as possible.

"What's wrong Ra?" Sean asked confused. He was just starting to get in his groove when Raquel suddenly stopped.

"Man, my agent is here! I was supposed to go meet him and I'm in here fucking round wit' you!" She shrieked as she rushed into the kitchen to grab her things and meet Charles at the front door.

As Raquel flung open the front door there was Charles, standing on her doorstep about to ring the bell.

"Oh! Hey Charles. I was just running out to meet you. Sorry I'm late again. It's just a lot going on," Raquel said trying to justify herself.

Charles wasn't trying to hear it. He didn't care one bit what was going on. Ever since they got back from LA Raquel hadn't been herself. He was tired of wasting his time with her lately.

"Whatever yo. Let's just get this over wit' so I can go. We'll talk about all this other bullshit later." Charles said as he gently pushed Raquel from in front of the door and entered the house.

Before Raquel could stop him, Charles was walking through the door. There wasn't anything she could do, she was caught red handed. Sean was still standing there in his boxers and pants around his ankles.

"So this is what you put me on hold for?" Charles turned around incredulously.

Raquel was at a loss for words. She had no idea of what to say. "I'm sorry. It's not what you think," she tried to explain.

"Not what you think? Fuck you mean? This ya new nigga or something? This bitch ass nigga?" Sean asked in disbelief, trying to figure out what the fuck was going on. He knew who Charles was but he didn't understand what all the hostility was about.

Charles usually didn't let people get him out of character, especially when there was business to handle, but he wasn't going to let any man disrespect him. He dropped his briefcase and rushed over to Sean, hitting him with a quick two piece.

Sean wasn't expecting that at all. He always looked at Charles as if he was a lame. Sean swung back, connecting with

Charles's chin. Raquel quickly ran over trying to break the two men apart.

"STOP! What the fuck are y'all doing?!" Raquel shouted. Things were spiraling more and more out of control. Now her personal life was clashing with her career and she had to do something to stop it.

Keisha heard all the commotion and came running out her room. "What's going on?" She hit the bottom step she saw Raquel in the middle of a tussle between Sean and another man she never met before. She went over to try to help her friend and was hit in the crossfire. Keisha yelled out in pain as she hit the floor.

"OK!!! THAT'S ENOUGH! Sean get out!" Raquel said wanting to end the drama. Sean caused enough damage in her life. Plus Keisha was already hurt and she didn't need any more traumas.

"You gonna take this nigga side?" Sean asked with a confused look on his face. Raquel didn't even look his way, she just pointed towards the door as she helped Keish off the floor.

"Are you ok boo?" she asked helping her friend up.

"Yea I'm fine but bitch are you ok? I heard all the noise upstairs."

Raquel couldn't even explain everything in front of Charles. She would have to talk to Keish about it later. "Yea I'm good. This is my agent Charles. Charles, this is my friend Keisha, the one I had to help the other night."

Charles fixed himself and walked over to shake Keisha's hand. He felt bad for being upset with Raquel for leaving. It was obvious Keisha needed her help just from looking at her bruised body. Still, he just caught Raquel with Sean so he didn't know what to think.

"It's nice to meet you Keisha. Sorry we had to meet this way. Are you ok? I didn't mean for anyone else to get hurt." Charles said feeling silly. He was a grown ass man, a businessman and here he was fighting like a street nigga in Raquel's beautiful home.

"Yes, I'm fine thank you. I will let you two talk, I'll be upstairs if you need me Ra. Nice to meet you Charles." Keisha said as she excused herself.

Raquel wasted no time trying to explain. She didn't want Charles to be upset, but it was already too late.

"Charles, I'm so sorry. It's not what it looks like. He was here when I came to drop Keisha off. He was talking and I got held up." She felt bad for lying to Charles but she couldn't admit the truth.

Charles didn't say a word. He simply picked up his briefcase and took a seat at the table. Raquel wasn't sure what was going through his head but she knew he wasn't happy with her at all right now.

"You gonna come sit down or you gonna keep wasting my time?" Charles asked. He was infuriated but he was going to keep his cool. Once they completed the assignments they already had in progress, he was going to drop her as a client.

Raquel slowly walked over and sat down at the table with Charles. He pulled the contract out his briefcase and began discussing the new and final offer on the table. He started the meeting off without missing a beat. He wasn't going to let Raquel's personal issues interrupt how he handled his business.

"So we got an offer for you to be part of a calendar shoot that will take place in the Bahamas. There will be twelve different women from twelve different countries, one representing each month. There will be a closed set, all expenses paid plus compensation. You wit it or what? I don't have time for you to think on it, I been trying to set this meeting up with you all day. If you not interested I can replace you." Charles spoke casually. Whether she took this gig or not no longer mattered to Charles.

He already had another model in mind he planned on making the next big thing.

Raquel was ecstatic about the offer! She never had this much of an opportunity but she was also afraid that her career was in jeopardy. She had to do exceptionally well on this gig and try to repair the damage she caused.

"That sounds great! When do we leave?" Raquel asked excitedly, trying to change the mood of the conversation. She was more than pleased with the offer and couldn't wait to get there. She had never been to the Bahamas before.

Charles was not moved by Raquel's upbeat demeanor not one bit. He was ready to get this over with and cut all ties with her.

"*You*," he corrected, "will be leaving tomorrow at twelve noon arriving in Nassau around 2:40pm and the shoot will be first thing the next morning."

"Ok… sounds good. When will you get there?" Raquel asked as she signed the contract.

Charles was tired of all the questions. He just wanted to get the contract signed and go home.

"You can take ya homegirl or Sean for that matter, but whatever you do make sure you take care of business and don't fuck up!" He replied, ignoring her question. "Oh, and be prepared for a video chat with Jacquelyn when you get back. I'll holla at you." Charles said as he gathered the paperwork, leaving Raquel's itinerary and plane tickets behind as he left out the door.

***

Sean left Raquel's house lost and confused once again. Just as he thought he and Raquel were off to a good start, she flipped like a light switch and threw him out. There was no way she could be fucking her agent or was it?

Sean's mind was filled with all types of thoughts as he drove downtown to his new home. He had finally accepted that he was going to be a father and was actually looking forward to it. While he was out yesterday buying odds and ends for the house, he also picked up a beautiful wooden crib that also had a matching bassinet and changing table as well. Once things cooled down between him and Keema he would invite her over so she could see it. He wanted to give her some time to deal with them not being together before he did so. Sean also wanted to bring Raquel over and show her the new place as well. He hoped they could make new memories here together as family.

Sean pulled into the garage, parked his vehicle and walked into his new domicile. He caught the elevator up to the fourth floor where his master suite was, and he felt like a king. He never knew a condo could be so luxurious. He always thought they were just a step up from an apartment but he was clearly wrong.

He rolled himself a blunt and went out on his balcony to look out at his city. He had to figure out a way to let Raquel know he was serious about her and their relationship. He sat there thinking and thinking until it finally hit him.

"I'll buy her a promise ring!" Sean spoke aloud to himself, proud that he'd come up with that idea on his own. He knew they weren't anywhere near ready to be married but he figured a promise ring was the perfect way to show his commitment. First thing in the morning he would get up and go ring shopping.

Sean walked back inside the condo feeling like all his problems were solved. He found a new home, he made things right with Keema, and tomorrow he would have Raquel back on his side. Nothing could steal his joy at the moment. He was back on top.

***

Raquel couldn't believe how her beautiful day of relaxation, food and drinks could turn into this. Once again her career was moving along but yet her personal life was full of nothing but drama.

Raquel went upstairs to go check on Keisha. She softly knocked on the door and waited for her to answer.

"Come in!" Keisha shouted as she lay in the bed watching television.

"You ok?" Raquel asked as she entered the room and sat on the bed beside her. She wanted to share the good news with Keish but once again her good fortune was being overshadowed by the mess she created.

"Yea. I'm good. What about you? What happened down there?" Keisha asked confused as hell.

Raquel really didn't feel like getting into the details. She would have to start from the beginning from when she and Charles messed around in L.A so she just gave the short version. "I missed my meeting with my agent fucking wit Sean so he's pissed off. I do have some good news though."

Keisha felt bad for not warning Raquel that Sean was coming over. She had no idea it would cause this type of drama. Since her and Raquel's friendship just got back to a good place, she wasn't going to mention anything and risk it.

"Well, what's the good news? Whateva it is you don't look so happy about it." Keisha stated.

"We going to the Bahamas tomorrow so we gotta go get ya stuff early. Is Dre gonna be at the house?" Raquel asked not acknowledging Keisha's comment.

"More than likely but I can wait till y'all come back. I'll just go shopping or steal some of ya clothes." Keisha said trying to make Raquel laugh which didn't work.

"No, you going with me." Raquel corrected. "You still got ya passport right?"

When Raquel said "we" Keisha had no idea she meant her. She figured she was referring to herself and Charles.

"Hell yea I still got it! You for real though?" Keisha asked excited as a kid on Christmas.

Seeing her friend so happy made Raquel crack a smile. She knew that she would always have a friend in Keisha even through their ups and downs.

"Yea I'm serious! I got booked to do a project out there and my agent ain't going so he said I can take you instead." she explained.

Keisha was so happy; she was in desperate need of a vacation. "I can't wait yo I'm so excited." Keisha said smiling from ear to ear.

"Listen though, I got an idea. I say we get some revenge before we go." Raquel suggested. All the madness was starting to push Raquel's mind into a deep dark place. All the anger and frustration she was holding in was about to force her to explode.

Keisha looked at her friend strangely. She hadn't heard Raquel speak like this in years. Sure, when they were younger nothing was off limits. If you did something to them they were sure to get you back, but as Raquel got older and started to blossom she left a lot of the street life behind.

"Revenge? Revenge on who? Wassup wit' you yo?" Keisha asked becoming concerned. She had no idea what was going through Raquel's mind.

"You said Dre is gonna be home right? I say we go in there, rob him and then pistol whip the fuck outta him!" Raquel suggested with a crazed look in her eyes.

Keisha was caught off guard. She didn't know where all this was coming from. She knew Ra was upset for what he did to her but this wasn't who Raquel was.

"Yo, are you crazy because you sound like it?" Keisha said looking her up and down.

Raquel wasn't crazy, nowhere near it but she was fed up. She wanted to take her anger out on someone and Dre was the perfect candidate.

"I'm not crazy. I'm just pissed off. He fucked you up so why can't we fuck him up?" she countered.

Hearing those words cut Keisha deep. She thought of all the trauma and pain she had endured through the years and then something in her switched.

"Why wait till the morning? Let's go get that nigga now." Keisha said now sharing the same crazy look Raquel sported on her face.

The two women went down the hall to Raquel's room and began to come up with a plan.

Chapter 11

Raquel went into the closet and pulled out her .45 caliber pistol from the closet as Keisha rolled a blunt for them.

"We won't need this." Raquel said as she removed the magazine and tossed it into the closet.

"So what's the plan Ra?" Keisha asked slightly nervous.

Raquel wasn't really sure what the plan was. She just wanted to get Keisha's stuff and have some fun while doing so.

"I don't know. It's ya house. I figured I leave that up to you. Is there another way for us to get in the house quietly besides the front door?" Raquel questioned trying to put the pieces of the puzzle together.

"Yea we can just slip in through the basement door." The lock has had been broken for over a year. Keisha kept trying to tell him to get it fixed but he never listened to her.

"This time of night he'll be upstairs in the bed sleep." Keisha added.

"Ok. Well that settles it. We'll go in through the basement, sneak upstairs and then attack!" Raquel shouted sounding like a military sergeant.

The two women threw on some comfortable clothes that were easy to move in, loaded up in the BMW and headed for Keisha's old home.

As Raquel and Keisha made their way into town, they reviewed the plan while smoking the blunt Keisha rolled to ease any rattled nerves. Raquel was more anxious than anything. She was rather calm during their conversation.

"Maybe we shouldn't park the car near the house." Keisha suggested as Raquel passed her the blunt as she switched from lane to lane.

"Yeah I thought about that. We gonna park around the corner in the alley. That way no one will see us." Raquel said trying to make sure every piece of their plan was flawless.

It sounded good and all but the more Keisha thought about it, the more nervous she became. She had developed a fear of Dre over the years and she didn't want him coming after her or Raquel.

"Well, Dre is gonna see our faces so what difference will that make?" Keisha asked rethinking her decision as she inhaled the smoke.

"Oh don't worry baby girl. I got everything under control. I got two ski masks in the back. Me and Sean use to use them when we went paintballing." As Raquel spoke, she noticed her friend's leg shaking.

Keisha did want her revenge on Dre but she didn't want to get hurt or caught in the process. "I'm just a lil' nervous that's all. This is starting to seem ridiculous. Let's just get my things in the morning and forget about this."

Keisha was trying to back down but Raquel wasn't trying to hear it. She had her thoughts set on the beautiful potent plant she would rob him for. She felt like Dre deserved this and it was going to happen.

"Don't worry nothing is gonna happen. We're gonna be in and out. That nigga is not expecting nothing like this, especially not from us. Look, all you have to do is get ya shit, I'll take care of Dre." Raquel instructed.

Keisha didn't know what to say. Her friend was acting like she was part of the damn mob or something. "Bitch, you been hanging out with Sean too damn long." Keisha rolled her eyes.

Within the next ten minutes the ladies were pulling up in the alley near Dre's house. There wasn't anybody out on the block, everything was nice and quiet just like they needed it to be.

Raquel grabbed the ski masks from the back seat giving one to Keisha.

"Leave ya phone and anything else that will make noise in the car. I'll take the remote off my keys and put it in my pocket so we can get back in the car. Oh and don't put ya mask on till we closer to the house." Raquel barked, placing her gun in her waistband.

The two women quickly went over the plan and hopped out with one thing on their mind—sweet revenge.

As they crept through the alley and over to Dre's backyard, they finally slip on the ski mask and crept over to the house. When they walked up to the basement door, Raquel stopped to make sure Keish was ready.

"Alright. I'll go in the door first. Wait till I knock him out before you run in to grab ya stuff. And bitch if shit gets sticky don't leave me hanging, alright?"

Keisha shook her head in agreement and swallowed her fears. She knew there was no turning back now. Raquel turned the doorknob and carefully opened the basement door. She made sure to keep the door open so they could make a quick and easy escape. Raquel took Keisha by the hand and led her upstairs.

As they neared the top of the steps Raquel peeped out the door before stepping out the basement and there was Dre. He was sitting in the living room watching television facing the basement door!

Did he see the door open? Raquel thought. "Bitch I thought you said he was gonna be sleep?!" she hissed.

Keisha was scared stiff. She didn't know what to do. Her first instinct was to run down the basement stairs and out the door but she didn't want to make too much noise and alert Dre.

"Shh! Bitch, I hear him coming!" Keisha whispered back in a panic. She didn't know what was about to happen. Here she was with her stupid ass best friend in ski mask like they were criminals. If Dre opened that door and found them there she didn't know he would do.

***

Charles laid in his bed unable to sleep. All he could think about was Raquel. He couldn't believe how naive he was but he was also glad he dodged a bullet. He was ready to give Raquel his all, show her what a good man really looked like and he just figured out she wasn't worth it. If Raquel wanted to be with a street nigga instead of him, than he would let her do exactly that.

He couldn't understand why all his choices in woman always turned out to be bad decisions. He didn't just judge women off their looks. He did love a beautiful lady but he looked for other qualities as well. He wanted a woman who was smart, hardworking, kindhearted, and generous. He thought he'd seen all those things in Raquel but now he was seeing another side or her he didn't like at all.

Even though he told himself he was done with Raquel, after having some time to unwind and think it over, he was reconsidering his decision. He did promise her if things didn't go well between them personally her career wouldn't suffer. Charles was a man of his word, but Raquel was also causing issues on the business side as well. If she proved herself on this trip he would consider making her his main client again.

In all honesty she was the best he had. Not to say the other women on his roster weren't just as good but Raquel, she was great. He also thought about giving her a chance to explain the situation with Sean. Like he told her in LA, you can't be mad at things that happened prior to you coming in someone's life. Plus it would put their working relationship back in a good place.

Charles got up and looked at his email to confirm the changes for his trip were made. Instead of flying to the Bahamas on the same day as Raquel, he would fly in the morning of the shoot. He also booked a room at another hotel. It was a little further away from the location of the photo shoot but he would just have to catch a taxi. He wasn't going to allow the personal issues with Raquel interfere with this trip, they would discuss things when they had some free time.

***

Dre sat in the living room watching TV when he noticed the basement door creep open. He wasn't sure if he was tripping from the pain pills he was on or if the door really did just open and close on its own. He was in too much pain to get up and investigate. He could barely sleep these days. Sean dislocated his jaw and he felt terrible. He also missed his wife Keisha. Dre wished he hadn't mistreated her all these years but he did, and there was no way he could make up for it. He knew Keisha was gone for good this time. She hadn't come back home or called him. That had never happened before.

Dre went back to watching TV and a few minutes later glanced back at the basement door. He was beginning to feel paranoid and wanted to know what made that door open up. He never noticed the door do that before. At least not that he could remember.

Dre slowly got up and walked over to the basement door to check it out. He stopped and put his ear to the door, listening for any noise or movement. Everything seemed normal but he opened up the door just to be sure. Dre felt a draft coming from downstairs so he went to check the broken door to make sure it was closed properly.

As he walked further and further down the basement stairs, he realized the basement door was wide open. Dre instantly started to panic. No breeze or wind could push the door open, even with the lock being broken. Dre hit the bottom step and reached for the light switch and Bam! He was knocked out like a light.

***

As Keisha and Raquel heard Dre approach the basement door they quickly and quietly walked back down the steps and hid behind the staircase. As he opened the door Keisha began to shake nervously. Raquel was scared shitless too but she held her composure, they didn't come here for nothing. Plus they had to be prepared for a fight if Dre found them.

As he hit the last step, Raquel came from out the shadows and cracked him upside the head as hard as she could with the gun. Dre hit the hard concrete floor and was instantly knocked out cold and Raquel noticed how fucked up Dre's face was. She was starting to wonder if there was more to the story than her friend told. *Maybe Keisha already got revenge and that's why she's so nervous.* They must have had a brawl because they both look liked they just returned from battle.

As Dre laid there on the floor barely breathing, both women froze. They had no idea of what to do next.

"Yo, just hurry up and go get as much stuff as you can. Where's his stash?" Raquel asked eager to get something out the deal.

"He has a safe in the bedroom. I watched him put the combo in a few times. Come on, let's go!" Keisha said as she turned to follow Raquel up the stairs. "Ahh! Help me!" she yelled as she hit the floor hard.

Raquel turned around, scared for not only Keisha but for the both of them.

***

Dre laid there on the floor pretending to be unconscious. He was completely confused. He had no idea who could be in his home attacking him like this. That was until the perpetrators began to talk and he couldn't believe his ears. Did Keisha and Raquel really think they could get over on him?

Dre slowly opened one of his eyes to get a glimpse and noticed neither woman had their attention focused on him. So as they tried to escape upstairs, he grabbed Keisha by the ankle pulling her down to the ground.

There was no way he was gonna let them leave out of there with anything that belonged to him. He was also going to teach Raquel a lesson just like he taught Keisha. He didn't care if Sean came back for him. Next time he would be prepared.

***

As Raquel heard Keisha yell out for help, she turned around to see what was going on. Keisha was on the floor and Dre was bleeding from the back of his head, scrambling to get up. He had a strong hold on Keisha's leg and Raquel automatically went into protectant mode. She ran over and kicked Dre in the head. The blow to the face caused him to let go of Keisha.

"Ahh! You fucking bitch! I'mma beat you like I beat ya friend!" Dre threatened Raquel, and she snapped.

"Move!" she shouted at Keisha, not wanting her to get hurt by being in the way. Raquel jumped on top of Dre like a mad woman pistol whipping him as if she were beating on a drum.

"STOP, RA! THAT'S ENOUGH LET'S GO!" Keisha yelled out.

Raquel continued to hit Dre and she didn't stop until she heard the gun go off.

POW!

Raquel jumped back dropping the gun.

"Oh my god! You shot him!" Keisha cried out hysterically. Raquel stood up in a daze, unable to comprehend what she just did. In a blind rage she just accidently killed a man.

"Oh my God! What are we going to do? I thought you said you just wanted to hurt him not kill him. You were supposed to take the bullets out!" Keisha cried.

Raquel was in shock. She had taken out the clip but didn't check the chamber. She couldn't believe she was so careless.

"I'm sorry. It-It was an accident. This wasn't supposed to happen." Raquel said as she paced back and forth. She had to figure out something and quick! She knew there was a possibility someone heard the gunshot and called the police. Now that she thought about it, her car looked very suspicious parked in the alley. "Think Raquel think." She spoke out loud, trying desperately to come up with something.

Keisha just stood there looking at the hole in Dre's face. Something in her was a bit sad. He *was* the man she was in love with. She felt like he deserved some type of punishment for the things he did, but death? That seemed a bit cruel. After all they still had their lives.

"Ok, so I got it. We go upstairs hit the safe and leave. Don't take nothing else out the house but ya passport." Raquel coached her friend.

Keisha couldn't believe after everything that just happened, Raquel was still worried about getting weed. None of that was important to Keisha right now. She just wanted to get out if there before the police came.

"Are you serious? We gotta get the fuck outta here! I'm not worried about no fucking weed and a couple of dollars." Keisha said with an attitude. She didn't want any parts of this.

Raquel was getting pissed off. She understood they were in a bad position and needed to get out of the house but they also needed to make this look good. Time was running out and there was no room for this.

"Bitch, use ya brain. It's not just about the weed. It's about making this look like a robbery gone bad. If you leave all ya shit here and the police come questioning you, you just tell them you ain't been back here since he beat ya ass and you don't knows what the fuck is going on!" Raquel shouted.

Keisha didn't know if that was going to work but there was no time to argue. She ran upstairs and Raquel followed right behind her. They were careful not to touch anything, using their sleeves to cover their fingertips.

Keisha grabbed her passport off the dresser and darted over to the safe. She entered the combination and boom, they were in. Keisha couldn't believe her eyes. She had no idea Dre had this much money stashed away. She grabbed all the bundles of cash and stuffed them into her pocket, bra, and underwear while Raquel grabbed a plastic bag off the floor. She took the bags of weed and his scale from the safe. After the woman collected everything, they darted back down into the basement ready to make a run for it.

Before leaving out of the house, Raquel carefully looked around to see if there were people outside after possibly hearing the gunshot. One good thing was she didn't hear any sirens so that told her no one called the police just yet.

"Come on!" Raquel said, running out the door and into the alley where her car was parked. She dug in her pockets for the remote, unlocked the car door and peeled off once she and Keisha were safely inside. As the turned onto the main road, Raquel slowed down not to bring attention to herself. It was after three in the morning and a nice car driving erratically on

Edmonson Avenue would definitely be suspicious in the eyes of the law.

She opened up the secret compartment, tossed in the gun and one of the bags of weed.

"Damn it, there's not enough room!" Raquel yelled slamming the compartment shut. Just then a police officer came zooming right up behind them.

***

Keema lay in the bed tossing and turning, she just could not get comfortable. She was still thinking about the conversation she had with Sean earlier that morning and it was still bothering her. Keema couldn't believe she actually had thoughts of keeping a baby she knew she didn't want. She only wanted the baby if that meant keeping Sean, and he made it perfectly clear that he wasn't going to be with her regardless if they had a baby or not. So, Keema decided to have an abortion and ruin his life instead. Nothing else in this world would make her happier.

Keema picked up the phone and dialed Sean's number not knowing if he would answer her call or not. She waited and waited until the answering machine picked up. She tossed the phone down on the bed, pissed that he didn't answer. She got up and walked over to her bedroom window, looking up at the stars.

She reflected on her life wondering how she made it this far. Keema made so many mistakes in her life and wished she grew up with someone to guide her. She always dreamed of being a social worker as a child so she could help kids who lived in foster homes like she did, but she got lost somewhere along the way. She never had a foster family that accepted her. Once she did something they didn't like, the family would send her right back. She always felt unwanted throughout her life and Sean was making her feel any different.

Her thoughts were interrupted by the sound of her phone ringing. She rushed over to the bed and saw that it was Sean. She answered the phone in a hurry, not wanting Sean to hang up.

"Hello?" Keema said anxiously.

"Is everything ok? You alright?" Sean asked. He was slightly worried. It was late and Keema sounded as if something was bothering her.

Keema was battling herself. On one hand she was still in love with Sean and wanted to fight for him, but on the other, he had hurt her and made it perfectly clear it was over so really there was nothing left to fight for. She took a deep breath before speaking, remembering her goal to get back at him.

"I just wanted to let you know I decided to have an abortion. I don't want this baby. That's all. Have a goodnight!" Keema said before disconnecting the call.

She felt a great sense of relief. For once in her life she was taking control. She was tired of selling herself short in order to please others. Keema would turn over a new leaf and without the help of Sean or any other man.

"If Sean wants to have a baby he better ask Raquel, but once I'm done with him, I'm pretty sure she won't want anything to do with him," Keema spoke to herself followed by a devilish laugh. She wasn't done destroying Sean's life just yet. She had one more surprise in store for him.

***

Sean couldn't believe it. Just when he was starting to accept the pregnancy and was looking forward to being a good father, Keema snatched the dream right from under him. Sean tried calling Keema back to back so they could talk about her decision but each time he was directed to the voicemail.

"Damn!" Sean yelled throwing his phone across the room. He couldn't understand why this was happening to him. He was starting to lose control once again. He went downstairs to the third floor where he had already picked out a room for the baby.

He stood there looking at the empty crib realizing no one would occupy it. Even though Sean didn't like the idea of Keema being the mother of his child, it happened and now he learned she would be killing a part of him. Sean didn't know what to do.

He left out the room and returned to his suite and stared out the window. This was the first time in his life that he felt defeated. He had lost Raquel and now the child he was preparing for would never come.

Sean sat there for the rest of the night with a million things running through his mind, unable to fall back asleep.

Chapter 12

The cop raced right up to Raquel's bumper and quickly swerved into the next lane, barely missing her. Raquel and Keisha both let out big sighs of relief as he flew past them. They thought they were caught for sure.

"Fuck, man! I hate when they do that. I was scared as shit!" Raquel confessed.

Keisha sat in the passenger seat quiet as a mouse. She was terrified and all she wanted to do was go home and hide out.

"You ard over there Keish?" Raquel asked noticing how afraid she looked.

Of course Keisha wasn't ok. She had just witnessed her husband be killed and now she was feeling like a criminal on the run.

"What are we gonna do yo? What if someone saw us?" Keisha asked frantically, starting to panic.

All of Keisha's nervous energy was starting to rub off on Raquel. She was making her more and more paranoid by the minute. One thing was for certain, they had a solid alibi. Raquel was going to the Bahamas regardless of what just happened. She wasn't going to ruin her career. Plus it also served as the perfect escape.

"Look Keish, I know things didn't go as planned and you're scared… I'm scared too but we have to keep a cool head and relax. We have to come up with a story and stick to it. We can go home and talk it over and try to get some sleep. In the morning, I'll take you shopping and we'll get on the plane." Raquel shrugged coolly. "We continue with our trip as normal."

Keisha sat there in a daze. As far as she was concerned she was fucked either way. She was his wife, she lived there with him, and she would be the first person they would come after. She really wished she thought this through beforehand.

The twenty minute ride seemed like an eternity. Every car that got too close to them made Raquel fear it was the police. They were relieved as they finally arrived home. She grabbed the contents out the compartment and entered the house. Both women decided they would go shower and meet back in Raquel's room.

Keisha went into her room and cried her eyes out. She couldn't believe what just happened. *How did things go so wrong?* She removed all the bundles of money she had stashed on her, peeled off her sweaty clothes, and hopped in the shower trying to wash away the memories of tonight. All she wanted to do was take it all back but it was impossible to reverse the hands of time. She just couldn't erase the picture of Dre's dead body on the cold, hard floor.

Keisha finished showering and laid down on the bed deep in thought. Raquel was her friend and she loved her, but she wasn't going to take the fall for this. Something had to give.

Down the hall, Raquel stood in the closet looking at the gun in her hand. She couldn't believe how things went so far.

"What the fuck were you thinking about?" Raquel asked herself. She had to try to think of a story line to rehearse with Keisha just in case any detectives or cops showed up. She cleaned off the gun and stuck it back in the box before hopping in the shower. After she got out Raquel went and sat on the bed and yelled for Keisha.

"Ok. So what's the plan?" Keisha asked sounding depressed as she walked into the room.

Raquel wasn't sure if Keisha was upset about the incident itself or if she was upset that Dre was now dead. There was no way she could feel bad for him after all he did to her.

"Well like I said, we go to the Bahamas as planned. That way we'll be exactly where we're supposed to be. It was Charles' idea for me to take you with me so there's someone to vouch for us without even knowing what's going on." Raquel began explaining.

She didn't want to put Charles in this middle of this but she had to worry about herself right now. "The only thing we can do is wait it out and see if any heat comes our way. If so we'll tell the cops everything that happened since Mo's up until tonight. After Charles left here we went to sleep to prepare for our trip the next day."

It sounded ok to Keisha but it wasn't solid enough. They needed something more. She sat there with a blank stare when it hit her like a ton of bricks.

Sean! He could be the decoy! She thought. *After all, he did go over there and beat the shit out of Dre. If things closed in on us, then he can be our outlet.*

"I got an idea." Keisha started tentatively, not knowing how Raquel would take her suggestion. "You may not like it but we gotta do what we gotta do. This *was* supposed to be about revenge, right?"

"Yea… wassup?" Raquel hesitantly asked.

"Well, Sean told me he went over to the house and beat up Dre. If they question us then we'll put the heat on him."

Raquel was upset with Sean but she wasn't sure if she wanted to set him up for murder. Even though there was no physical evidence to link Sean to the death of Dre, the justice system was fucked. There was a big possibility he could still go down for his murder if they implicated him. At the end of the day Raquel would rather it be Sean in the middle of a murder investigation and behind bars than her. She had way too much to lose.

Raquel took a deep breath and released it slowly before responding, "Well bestie, I think we just came up with our alibi."

Smiling, the two friends embraced, knowing that the days ahead of them would be rough.

***

The next morning Charles was awake early, ready to get his day started. He had a lot of preparing to do for the Bahamas. Even though he was still pissed with Raquel, he decided to shoot her a text reminding her of the importance of this gig.

GM today is the big day! Be on time, don't miss ya flight and NO DRAMA!

-Charles

He wanted everything to go smoothly. He didn't want Raquel's personal drama affecting his good reputation. Charles had to straighten out some things with some of his other clients and grab a few things for his trip so he began to prepared himself. The next few days for him would be absolutely beautiful. Nothing but sun, women, and money—what else could a man want? He ate a quick breakfast, showered and headed out the door.

***

Just as Sean dozed off he was awakened by the ringing of his cell phone. He was in no mood to talk to anyone. He was still very tired and very pissed off. Sean's phone rang continuously. Realizing that it wouldn't stop until he answered, he searched around for his phone. After following the sound, he found it in the corner with a cracked screen.

"Keema." He muttered seeing her name on the caller ID.

He had no idea what the fuck she was calling him for at eight o'clock in the morning, especially after she ruined his good night's sleep with her drama. Since she decided she was going to have an abortion, Sean decided there was nothing else for them to talk about.

Sean powered off his phone and went back to bed.

Keema tried calling Sean countless times but she was greeted by the voicemail each time.

"I can't believe he turned his phone off! That good for nothing bastard!" Keema shouted as she threw her up phone up against the wall, effectively shattering it into pieces.

"Fuck! Fuck!" was all Keema could say. She had no money, no car, and now no phone. She really felt all alone and the worse part of it all was her aunt just called to inform her Dre was found dead early this morning. Keema couldn't believe it. She and Dre just connected a little over a year ago after belatedly finding out they were related. Now, just like that, he was gone. Every time someone came into her life they left her in some kind of way. Keema felt all alone. She was really beginning to feel like she hit rock bottom.

Keisha and Raquel stayed up the whole night. Neither of them could sleep.

Raquel packed her bags while Keisha replayed the events over and over again in her head. The two of them also did some role playing, preparing for the good cop bad cop routine just in case things ever came to that.

They left the house bright and early so they could be one of the first people at Towson Mall when it opened at nine. All Raquel wanted to do was buy her friend some things and head straight to the airport. She was starting to get a little scared and wanted to get out of town ASAP.

After spending about an hour at the mall, the ladies headed back to the car and checked to make sure they had everything they needed before heading to the airport.

"Ok. I know shit is crazy and it's gonna be hard but let's try to put this behind us while we're in the Bahamas. Let's have a good time. We'll deal with this shit when we come back, and that's only *if* we have to." Raquel said giving Keisha a lil' pep-talked.

Keisha couldn't understand how Raquel could be so calm about this. All she could hope for was to return home without anyone pointing fingers at her.

"Ok. I'll try my best." Keisha agreed, putting on her shades.

Raquel put the car and gear and the ladies were off to the airport.

Sean woke up a few hours later feeling refreshed after getting some much needed sleep. The situations involving the women in his life were beginning to wear on him.

He picked up the phone and tried to call Keema back but no luck, just the answering machine. He waited a few minutes later before trying a second time and the same thing happened. At this point Sean was starting to worry. What if she was in the hospital or something? Sean jumped up, threw on some clothes, and headed to Keema's.

Sean made it to the house within ten minutes. He hopped out urgently, pounding on the door hoping everything was alright.

Keema came to the door crying and she looked terrible. Her eyes were red and puffy and her nose was running.

"Yo, what's wrong?" Sean asked walking inside the house and sitting Keema down on the sofa. She was so upset that she couldn't even get any words out. He ran to the kitchen to get her some water.

Keema took a sip and began to slowly clam down. She was glad that Sean came and she was no longer alone.

"Now tell me wassup? Is something wrong with the baby? It wouldn't matter though cause you ain't keeping it, right?" Sean said trying to make her feel guilty.

Keema was in no mood for him being an asshole right now. She could care less how he felt about the baby but when she heard about Dre, she didn't know who else to call.

"Dre is dead!" Keisha yelled out, sobbing even harder.

Dead? But I just saw him a couple of days ago, Sean thought to himself.

"Dead? What you mean?" he asked, trying to get clarity on the situation.

"His mom called me and told me he was found dead in the basement. She said the police found him dead after receiving a call about gunshots from the elderly neighbor next door. The detective said it looks like a robbery. It's funny how that bitch Keisha is nowhere to be found." Keema said wondering where the hell she was during all this.

"Damn. That's fucked up."

Sean wasn't sure if Keisha and Raquel knew because no one called him, but maybe they wouldn't have anyway. He wasn't Raquel's or Keisha's favorite person right now. He planned on calling Raquel later to see if she they heard anything, but for now he would stay and console Keema.

***

As Raquel and Keisha pulled into the parking garage, the women grabbed their things and headed to the shuttle. Once seated, the ride to the airport seemed to take forever. Raquel could envision being stopped by TSA and federal agents in connection with Dre's murder.

Fuck that, Raquel thought. *Nothing is going to happen.* She tried to erase those negative thoughts and act as if everything was normal.

Everything went smoothly when they entered the airport, allowing the girls a moment to finally relax. They boarded the plane, drifting off to sleep before takeoff.

Two hours and forty five minutes later they had arrived in beautiful Nassau. They caught a cab from the airport and to the hotel which was absolutely stunning. Raquel checked them into their rooms and headed towards the elevator.

They dropped Keisha's things off in the room that originally belonged to Charles, then went down the hall to Raquel's suite.

She found a note and a box left on the bed by hotel staff. She opened up the typed note and it was from Charles.

I had to pull a lot of strings for this, enjoy.

Raquel smiled to see the beautiful, hand carved wooden box was full of cigars and weed. Charles made sure to have someone deliver it to her. He wanted Raquel to have everything she needed to make sure this project was a success. She started to unpack a few things so she could take a shower but she decided to check her phone first. Raquel had a single text and it was from Sean.

Yo Keema told me Dre is dead. Does ya girl know? Call me I wanna make sure y'all alright.

-Sean

Raquel froze up with fear. She wasn't exactly sure if Sean knew more than what he was saying. *Did the police ask about Keisha? Did he tell Keema that Keisha is now staying with me?*

"What's wrong?" Keisha said, panicking as she saw the worry written on her friend's face.

"Oh my god bitch, we're fucked!" Raquel blurted out without thinking.

"What? What's wrong?" She knew it had to be something big from the look on Raquel's face. She just hoped it wasn't what she thought.

"Sean texted me while we were on the plane. He and Keema know Dre is dead. The police found him already." Raquel hung her head low. She thought they were in the clear but just like that things took a turn for the worse.

"What? Are you serious? What else did he say?" Keisha asked frantically, scared out her mind. She knew something would happen and she would be the first person people would want to contact whether they thought she had something to do with it or not.

"Nothing, he just asked if we were ok. I don't think they suspect anything. I don't know why I said that." Raquel said regretting her choice of words.

Keisha was fuming! *How did I let Raquel get me into this mess?* "Look bitch, we cool and all but I'm not going to jail over this! You need to figure this out!" Keisha stressed, slamming the door behind her as she left the room.

Raquel had to admit she was scared of what could happen. She had no idea if anyone saw them or her car for that matter. If anyone got a look at her license plate then they definitely had something to worry about. Being spotted at the scene of the murder would totally comprise everything.

Raquel went into the bathroom and filled up the tub with hot steamy water. She really needed to relax and think things through. She wasn't sure what Keisha met by her comment but Raquel knew one thing for sure: If they returned home and things got bad for the two of them, and *if* Keisha turned on her, then her dear friend just might meet the same fate as her late husband.

Until then Raquel was going to play her cards right to make sure no matter what happened she stayed out of jail. She would make sure someone else would take the fall for Dre's murder, even if that meant framing Keisha...

Stay tuned for part two, coming fall of 2014…

Acknowledgements

Thank you to all my family and friends who have supported me and my dreams throughout the years. You guys have been my inspiration.

I would also like to say thank you to one of the greatest people in the world, my good friend Jamie. This book wouldn't have happened if it weren't for you. It all started when you suggested that I finally give writing a try after years of contemplating and so I did. I never expected it to become what it is today and I'm so grateful for all the help and guidance you have given me along the way. You encouraged me and kept me going during the times I wanted to quit or I was just being plain lazy.

Most importantly you believed in me and my talent as a writer more than I believed in myself. You are truly a blessing in my life, and no matter how many miles are between us you have always been a good friend and I love you dearly. (P. S We need to get back into the same state lol)

And last but not least, my readers! I love you the most, you are the reason I am here!! Stay tuned for part two!!!

Also, don't forget to visit http://eepurl.com/NzLlH to be added to Self-Made Publishing's mailing list for exclusive sneak peeks, contests, and more!

--Déjá Monét

You Can Reach Me At:

Twitter: @AuthorDejaM

Facebook: Self Made Publishing

Instagram: AuthorDejaM

Cover Model Instagram: _LailaZoe

Email: Selfmadepublishing@gmail.com